Helmets

Morven Moeller

DreamPunk Press

Copyright © 2025 by Morven Moeller

All rights reserved.

No portion of this book may be reproduced in any form without written permission from the publisher or author, except as permitted by U.S. copyright law.

This is a work of fiction. The actions and words of the characters are strictly figments of the author's imagination, and any resemblance to actual events, places, and persons, living or dead, is entirely coincidental.

No portion of this book is to be used in training or data banking for Artificial Intelligence without written permission from the author.

No portion of this book was created using Artificial Intelligence.

ISBN: 978-1-963928-05-1
978-1-963928-06-0 (open dyslexic)
978-1-963928-07-5 (e-Pub)

Contents

1. Helmets   5
2. Mastermind   29
3. Goldfish   53
4. Jaywalk   87
5. Tether   115

IN NEWS AND UPCOMING EVENTS

Celebrating 10 Years of Alps in North Carolina

Covered by Kellem Hall, Independent Reporter
Reviewed by Jaxon Treau, Alps News and Blogs
Posted 2998 days ago, Last Edited 2993 days ago

Before the Alps Processing Center, life was very different in the Tidewater region, which includes south-eastern Virginia and most of eastern North Carolina. Hurricanes and rising waters had incentivized many families to seek higher elevation. For many residents, Hurricane Randy was the final straw, dealing about 135 million dollars' worth of damage across the region.

Alps CEO, Steven Benedict, announced the Greenville Processing Center during a hope-seeking mission to the area. The ubiquitous image most will remember from the news coverage featured Benedict in his red Alps-branded life jacket. The image itself doesn't offer anything to indicate where his visit had taken him, but we know now that it was to one of the hardest hit districts of Greenville. In the impromptu announcement, he said, "Alps will clean this all up. We will build a center and a community to house all the victims of Randy."

Following the announcement, Alps set up medical pop-ups, distributed ready-made meals and life vests, and made immediate job and property offers to the neighborhood residents. I spoke with a few of the original residents, asking them about what Alps' aid had meant to them during that difficult time. Henry Thomas was happy to speak with me about Alps, "I never did see Steven Benedict, but I just knew he'd been here. People were acting like people again, smiling and being friendly. Only a man like that could swoop in and really get things moving." Thomas even showed me the life vest he'd gotten when he first approached the Alps pop-ups, he chuckled, "Just in case we get another Randy."

These days, the probability of another Randy is difficult to calculate. The Corporate Council's Oceanic and Atmospheric Committee attributes that to Greener Pastures, a sustainability focused project backed by, then bought by Alps, which rapidly captures carbon and redirects excess heat from notorious polluters.

I asked Thomas and his partner Del what they thought of the work Greener Pastures had done in Suffolk-Franklin-Windsor (SFW) zone. <u>Their reviews were mixed</u>. But, Thomas thought the work was paying off, bringing more predictable weather and crop yields.

This month, the Greenville Processing Center kicks off their 10-year anniversary, planning various events and activities for processors, associates, community members, and families to participate in. If you drop by, look out for Henry and Del Thomas, or the 1300+ other original residents who still work at the center. A full schedule of activities is available on the Alps events page <u>here</u>.

Helmets

I WANTED TO THROW the phone across the room. "You're sure?" I wished Teena wasn't.

"I'm sure of it. Saw it myself." On the other end of the line, Teena had some broadcast playing in the background. It was loud enough that I could hear it. The news anchor was reporting a new food group that the school system planned to add to the menu. "He and Jarrod were walking back with the cat food, and they picked them up. Something about curfew."

"But the curfew isn't until 9," I seethed, pushing the words through gritted teeth. I flicked my eyes to the clock tile set into the kitchen backsplash. It read 9:02. "Fuck those bots."

Teena hummed. "I know that's right."

I needed to do something with my hands. I needed to tear something apart. I put my phone down carefully, making sure not to let my anger go unchecked in the moment of handling the thin piece of glastic. Once the fragile, polymer rectangle was on the counter, I tapped at the speaker button. "Didn't the mayor say that if you were on your way home then the rocops let you go home?" I pulled a head of cabbage from the fridge, unwrapped the waxy paper around it, then ripped the leaves off.

"That's what he says, but that's not what I saw." The news anchor had moved to another news story; this one was about biotic pollinators—called buzzers—melting during their migrations. "I saw two kids get stopped, helmetted, and taken away to the central facility." She sighed. "I thought about going out there, but there's nothing that says they wouldn't have just put me in one of them helmets too. Somebody's gotta be out here to pay the fine."

I was furious in a cold way and unsurprised in a hot way. I hadn't been sure what to expect of the rocops when they first were introduced, but I had known it wouldn't be good. While our area wasn't one of the pilot programs, it was one of the first places where it was instituted after the pilot ended. The pilot programs were in places like Louisiana, Florida, Texas; places where processing centers were already a booming economic successes. They also happened to be places that wanted perfectly obedient and scalable police forces, which was what the corporate contract had provided them.

Rocops weren't actually robots, but the processing helmets and bio armor precluded them from being people. In many ways, they were exactly the same as Jarrod and Nezzer. The steps they took swayed the same. The hands they used were blistered the same. But the words that fell from their mouths were wrong, chewed up by systems they were plugged into.

There was nothing I could do until the morning, after the curfews lifted.

●—●

"Did Nez get home?" Dad looked over to the empty chair to his left, across from me. "No," he answered himself, "his dishes would be there." He reached a slow hand over to the spot and ran his palm over the ridges of the placemat. "Where's Nez?" He turned his eyes - always a little glassy, always a little wet - toward me.

I chewed the bite of dinner in my mouth extra long, not because I had to think of what to say, but because I had to steel myself to answer. I swallowed harder than stewed cabbage necessitated. "Nez will be home tomorrow." I immediately followed my comment with another bite, this time of a mince-loaf seasoned beyond recognition.

Nodding along, Dad withdrew his hand. "I heard on the news that the smoke's getting worse. Nez shouldn't be out in that." He scooped some of the cabbage onto his spoon; the small gyroscopic device fit into his palm counter-acted his shakes as he did. His lips reached out to meet the spoon when it came up. He grinned, nodding at me, the only sign he was likely to give me that he enjoyed his meal.

Bringing up the helmets was never a good idea with dad. He'd spent fifteen years working at the Greenville Processing Center, back when it was daily shifts and honest work. Back then, my mom had her suspicions about exactly how honest it was, but it was hard to argue. The largest corporations, their news casts, their politicians, and their paid endorsements all revered the technological revolution. And it was hard to refute the claims, when no one who worked there could tell you otherwise.

Dad would leave, ride a share car for an hour to the processing center, work at the center for five hours, then ride the share car back. He'd burst through the door saying, "It's like I ain't seen you all day!" And he hadn't, but he always told us that working a processing shift was like a summer nap. You'd feel like you were dozing off, then you'd snap back awake. Even though it felt like no time had passed, you'd look up to the clock and see that your shift was over.

I used to wonder what it was like. I used to fidget when the other kids would say their parents had invited them to the family day at the center, but I had to tell them that I wasn't going, that my mama said I couldn't go. Fumi and James would plot with me, trying to find a way for me to sneak away, but my mama was always smarter than our plans. The last time we'd planned something, she threw my covers off me early in the morning on family day, packed me half-asleep into the local carpool, and took me to the cloth recycling plant. I had hated that day at the cloth plant. The masks had to be tight to our faces so that we wouldn't breathe in the fiber, and we had to wear protective gear over our eyes and ears too. I sat there, bored for hours, cursing my mama and plotting my escape.

Dad ate the last of his dinner. He dropped his fist to either side of his plate, a nightly ritual. "It ain't your mama's cooking." His gaze met the picture of mama on the wall. "She cooks like you, but you did it better." He grinned at her. "One day, we'll have dinner again."

Collecting the dishes, I took them into the kitchen, gifting dad with the same quiet moment with mom's portrait that I did every night. I scraped what was left on the dishes into the compost trap and set the plates into the wash cabinet. I considered taking Nez's clean plate out of it first, but with nowhere to put it in the meantime, left it there.

"Hey, Meela?"

I pressed the start button on the wash cabinet. "Yeah, dad?"

His walker jittered into the kitchen first, then he followed it, settling his hip into the curve of it. "Where's Nez? Did he get home?"

Taking a deep breath, I strode forward to help him turn his walker around to head back to the living room. "No," I said, trying to keep my tone even, "but he'll be back tomorrow." I helped to settle him into his chair.

"Ah." It wasn't clear if it was in response to the chair or his answer to me. His eyes fell into their usual spot, staring straight forward into the entertainment cabinet filled with mementos and trinkets on display, like his ten-year certificate and his Alps life jacket. I didn't think he was actually seeing them anymore, his eyes were glazed by a wetness and confusion that never went away. "I heard on the news that the smoke's getting worse."

I called out from work the next morning, knowing that the task ahead of Teena and I wasn't a quick one. When Dean went in to pay her son's fee, she'd been stuck in line for hours. She told our team about it the next day, said she had even considered leaving. It was just so much to stand in a room that long. The good news is that once she'd been seen by the clerk, it was super quick.

My and Teena's share car rolled into the Center's u-shaped carport structure, shielding us from the city's smoke. Just like Dean'd said, we had to put our devices into lockers in the atrium. I tucked my glastic phone into one of the thin locker slots, closed the door, and tugged the key out. The lockers lined the back wall of the atrium, hundreds - maybe thousands of them - with their mouths open wide.

I waited while Teena flicked through her apps. "I just gotta check a few things first." She flew through notifications and message screens, letting each application and each person know that she'd be away from her phone. Once she'd finished, she delicately placed it into a locker too. "Didn't you have to let someone know that you'd be away?"

Shaking my head, I headed toward the chemical detectors at the far end of the room. "Who would I tell?" The only people I messaged were my work team, Teena and her family, and Nezzer; all of whom were either already aware that I was here or unaware of the situation entirely.

We followed the signs into the building, which led is to a long hallway, decorated with articles from different news sites lauding the advancements that the processing centers had headed. With headlines like 'Less Crime and Better Benefits' and 'No More Long, Pointless Hours at Work' and 'Make a Difference Just by Showing Up'. Teena's eyes darted from plaque to plaque, frame to frame. "So, uh, who's watching your dad?"

Training my eyes on the door at the other end of the hallway, I kept marching forward. Something about the long empty hallway just didn't sit right with me. Something in my gut churned, like a throbbing in my temple making me sick to my stomach. "Sylvie." I managed. "She came over from next door. Used to be one of the city's home health workers before the NationAlive won that contract."

Teena stopped at one of the articles. "This one is about Englewood. You ever visited?"

I didn't let my eyes off the door, but I stopped to stand next to Teena, trying to shake my discomfort by swallowing hard. "No. We should get moving, though." I couldn't quite put my finger on it; there was a buzzing in the air, and it made the entire world seem further away than it was supposed to be. The gray walls were crawling at the edges of my vision, like when you're too high above sea level for comfort..

"I went with my cousin once. His husband worked at the processing center and had opted to live in one of the communities. It was so nice. They had pools and tennis courts, everything you could ever need to keep you occupied." Teena took two tiny steps forward to the next article on the wall and started to read it, her eyes moving slowly across the printed words.

I glanced at her, appalled by her pause. "Teena, let's get going." When Teena didn't move, I grabbed her by the wrist and started pulling. It was easy to do; she was pliant. I was not.

The door was smaller than it was supposed to be. From the other end of the hallway, it loomed, looking like it reached up, meeting the vaulted ceiling, but the closer we got, the more apparent the trick of the light was. All of the walls were the same gray, but the way the lights pointed and intersected with each other made everything seem grander than it was.

I grabbed the metal door handle and pulled, the door didn't budge.

"Oh darn. This place sure is confusing. We should go get help, maybe they aren't open yet." Teena turned to walk back down the hallway. She didn't seem to notice that the hallway was oscillating with a skull-rattling thrum.

My eyesight swam with the waves forcing my head to swirl. I held Teena's wrist tight. I squinted at the door, hoping it might focus my eyes through my throbbing head. My breathing picked up, and I could tell that I was freaking out, that my brain was going faster and faster, that I was going to faint or exhaust myself.

My mama always taught me to breathe my way through frustration, but even she didn't listen to her own advice. She usually followed dad's advice, humming something to keep her going. When she was cleaning the house, she'd hum a tune she remembered from when she was young. When she folded laundry, she'd hum a new song from the charts. Even when she worked at the cloth recycling plant, surrounded by earmuffs and breathing masks, her head would bob up and down, humming along to whatever was in her head. Dad would always say, "You can't be upset, if you're humming your favorite song."

With the world rattling loose at the edges, I started to hum. I hummed through a clenched jaw and flared nostrils, some song that my brother played on the surround system from his tablet. It was an old-timey tune with deep bass and fast lyrics, sewn together with emotion. I covered my ears and hummed louder, paying attention to my tune over the unraveling around me.

Teena looked at me, but in a blank way without concern, like she was watching me through a screen, like she wasn't also there.

As I hummed louder, I started to notice when the notes would drown out the noise, and I got better at it. Soon the tidal wave had simmered down into a tide pool, warm, full of nature minding its own business.

I squinted at the door again, and this time, I was able to force the metal into something more. The metal plate had grooves in it that caught the light at the worst angles. It said push. So, I wrapped my hand around the handle and reached back to grab Teena.

Teena wasn't there anymore. Still humming, I turned to look down the hallway. Teena stood at another of the plaques, looking over the words in a daze. She was inching further away, but my jaw hurt and my nose stung from humming in such an intense way.

The hand that had been reaching for Teena balled into a fist at my side, and I pushed the door open.

Serene. I choked on my humming; it felt far too loud and far too much for this new space. This room reminded me of an airport. Eerie, like it was made for more people than it should have been. There was a clerk window on the far side of the room. The helmeted clerk sat impossibly still, like most helmetted processors, waiting for the next person to approach.

No one did. There was a complex, cordoned maze set between the door and the window for queuing. And there were people waiting there, three people. They looked lost, staring into space or at the floor. One person seemed to be in a part of the queue that met a dead end. Why would a queue have a deadend?

I crouched down under the cords and walked through the queue, fairly certain that the clerk wouldn't mind and the other patrons wouldn't notice. "Hi, I'm here to pay the fee for a pick-up."

"Name," the clerk didn't move. They didn't have a screen or tablet; they didn't have anything but a chair, an empty desk, and their helmet.

"Who's name?" Did they want my name? Nez's name?

"Name," the clerk repeated.

"I'm here to pick up Kadnezzer Thomas."

"Kadnezzer Thomas is not available for release. They will be available for release starting today, processing times may vary."

Excuse me? "I'm here to pay the fee for his release."

"Kadnezzer Thomas's fee is not available. The fee schedule will begin at $10,000 in forty-seven minutes."

"Ten-thousand- What? No, I looked up the fee, and next-day pick up is less than $1000."

"Kadnezzer Thomas will be available for $1000 fee after a 24-hour processing time."

What? No. "He was picked up last night." I took time off from work that I couldn't get back; I'd paid for a share car that I couldn't get back. "I need to speak to someone."

"How can I assist you?" The clerk's monotone was unfazed by my frustration.

"A real person," I insisted, but I still felt a pang of guilt. Under that helmet was a real person, just like dad, just like Nez. I swallowed my emotion, but it kept coming back up, until I blurted, "I need to speak to someone who..." I waved a hand to the helmet, "who isn't connected to the processing system." After a beat, I added, "Now."

The motionless clerk continued to do absolutely nothing, sitting there in perfect posture. Perhaps, the clerk had run out of script, and they were processing the situation. I imagined some computer node in the facility coming to life, processing my input, for the first time. But that couldn't be right; I couldn't be the first person to ask. I turned my eyes to the people in the room behind me. They were stagnated like cloth soaking in the wash baths at the cloth recycling plant. The person who'd come to a dead end, was starting to move back toward the main path, slowly. "What's wrong with them?"

This question must've had a scripted answer. The clerk immediately responded, "Persons performing unscheduled processing, especially those who begin in a high emotional state, may experience lingering symptoms like anxiety, depression, exhaustion, hunger, diarrhea..."

I tried to block out the answer. It only made me worry about Nez. He'd never been processed. Just like I'd never been processed.

"... avoid unscheduled processing when you can, or submit calmly-"

"Submit calmly?" I turned to the paused clerk, who was so hard to ignore when the room was so empty and so quiet. "Submit calmly to having your brain hijacked by some corporate conglomerate?"

The clerk had a response for that too. "Processing is a secure occupation for many processors."

"Secure," I scoffed. Security was certainly one aspect of it. It was a secure job that wasn't going away. But it wasn't safe; it wasn't healthy. Processing had left my father unable to find the right words through overused neural pathways, unable to see through eyes that had likely dried out from a lack of blinking. Rodney, a man who lived down the street from me who would take care of the street cats and possums, said that the center must've changed something about the processing, since he didn't need his eye drops anymore. And while that was a good thing, and I was truly happy for all the people whose eyes wouldn't cloud over with cataracts in twenty years; what was going wrong that we couldn't see? What was the new health risk they'd find in twenty years, thirty? I furrowed my brow and turned back to the clerk, "You said that it's secure for many. Who isn't secure in their processing career?"

I thought I'd asked another answerless question, but after a long pause, the clerk found an answer. "Processing is a secure occupation." So, it was a question that the clerk wasn't allowed to answer.

My head fell back in something like defeat, staring at the ceiling. "What do I do while I wait for Kadnezzer to be done processing?"

"Please wait patiently. Processing times may vary."

Shaking my head, I closed my eyes. "Is there a person I can speak to who doesn't have a helmet on?"

"Hang on while I find an associate to assist you."

My eyebrows were fixed in a high position on my forehead. When I started to feel the strain in those muscles, I smoothed my expression down. "Why didn't you say so before?"

It felt like a long time because of the silence in the room, because every surface was a gray-off-white. Eventually, a handleless door behind the clerk swung open. An associate strode out. They wore a black t-shirt and jeans, but they were nicer than any t-shirt or jeans that my family had worn. I'd never seen a t-shirt and jeans that nice at the recycling plant either. People where I was just didn't have that kind of money. "Hi. I'm Jay and use he/him pronouns. How can I help you today?" He had light skin that looked pink in the dinge-colored room.

I cleared my throat. "I'm here to pick up Kadnezzer Thomas."

"Let's see. Thomas. Thomas." He pulled a glastic tablet from his back pocket, and started to flick through the information there. He wore a name tag with MR JAY LENDER. It seemed old-fashioned to include the title, but I'd never worked for a corporation, so maybe that's just how it was done. "Ah," he said, "It looks like he is still required to complete his initial processing. He should be available for pick up starting in a few minutes." He smiled wide. "The clerk can help you with the paperwork." He motioned to the clerk.

Sticking a hand on my hip, I pursed my lips. "The clerk says that I'll have to pay $10,000 dollars. I'm hoping you can help me with that."

He looked back down to his tablet and adjusted his glasses on his nose. "Well, the initial processing time is usually 12 hours, then the fee schedule starts at $10,000 for pick up."

"But when I looked it up, it said next-day pick up was $1000 or less." I motioned a flat hand in a circle. "It's the next day."

"When was he brought in?" He tapped at his tablet.

I didn't feel like being helpful. At this point, I felt like stomping my feet and crying, but I knew that I couldn't do either. "Why is this so difficult? It's the next day, so it should be $1000 or less." I pressed my lips together to stop myself from saying any more.

Jay was calm, which made me feel so much worse about the whole thing. He turned his tablet around to me. "Processing centers are open 24hrs, so we calculate everything by business hour. So, the file says that Thomas started processing at 9:07 yesterday evening," he glanced to me for confirmation.

I narrowed my eyes.

He continued as if I'd been entirely amenable, "Because of some difficulty with the processor, his processing speed was intermittent at first, but everything smoothed out soon enough." He swiped his finger to show me something else.

I'd been so focused on not being angry, I hadn't seen the first thing. I probably wasn't going to see the second thing either.

"And, that means his initial processing period should be coming to an end here soon. Then the fee schedule will apply. The options are to pay off the fee by working or for someone to pay the fee. The center is very generous, offering $1000 compensation for each of the first nine hours, then $100, then $10." He retracted his tablet and put it away. He watched her with an annoyingly pleasant face.

So, I'd have to wait at least nine hours before I could pay the fee. I flicked my eyes back to the other people in the waiting room. I thought about what Dean had said. Something still seemed off, but... I turned back to Jay; his stupid smile still plastered on his face. "So, you're saying I have to wait here for another 9 hours, before the price on the informational is correct."

His smile didn't falter. "It will be about nine hours before the fee schedule will be at a $1000 fee." He nodded.

"So, what am I supposed to do until then?" I tried not to think of the other people in line. I wasn't sure what was wrong with them, but I was sure that I couldn't help them. They were stuck in whatever trance the hallway had failed to put me in. And it seemed that Jay and I were bound to ignore it, since he wasn't and I sure as hell wasn't going to bring it up.

Jay's brow pinched together. "Have you ever taken a tour of a processing center?" He tapped at his tablet again. "Thomas family. So, your father used to work at the processing center, but it looks like no one from his immediate family has taken a tour with us. Would you like to take the tour?"

"Is there a better option?" I pursed my lips at him, really hoping there was.

With an 'ah-ha' expression, Jay tapped through his tablet. "If you wish, we could submit you to processing to help pay off the fee." He turned the tablet around, on the screen was a single large green button labeled 'I submit to processing'.

I slapped the tablet and Jay's hand away. "I'll take the tour."

THE URBAN GREENER

Forum Post: Remedies for TechnoBlah

Posted by Del Thomas, Naturalist and Mom
Reviewed by Bella Nickel, Alps Small Site Services
Posted 3395 days ago, Last Edited 3388 days ago.

As most of you know, and as most of you can relate to, my husband commutes to the processing center for processing shiftwork. He loves his job with Alps.

And like most shift workers, he works 4 shift days then has 3 rest days, but I'm interested to know if anyone else has seen a similar pattern for their loved ones. On his days off, my husband sits at the tv for almost 6 hours straight. Now, for some people, I understand that this is normal, but my husband has never liked to watch television, especially day programming, and has never enjoyed keeping still. At dinners, he's often bouncing his leg or tapping his fingers, playing some tune only he knows.

During his tv laze, he is almost motionless, eyes glued to the tv. Trying to get his attention is incredibly hard, too. He was cleared for work by Alps medical, no signs of depression or fatigue, but I don't want him cleared for work. I want him cleared for home. I have found that if I hide the remote and the tv remains off all day, then my husband continues his day in the ways he had before. He works in his garden and socializes with our neighbors. Is this happening with anyone else?

42 Comments. Top 5 Comments below. Del Thomas turned off commenting for this post.

Comment by Brant Kade (Site Admin)
Sunshine and gardening are great ways to ward off the TechnoBlah.

Comment by Jimmy Trust
Sounds like your husband needs his wife to lay off. He provides for his family. He deserves the screen time.

Comment by Del Thomas (Author)

He is allowed to do whatever he pleases, but I've known the man for 30 years. TV is not something he's interested in.

Comment by Jimmy Trust, Flagged by Admin and 5 others, Cleared by Bella Nickel

Bitch

Comment by Phoenix Rhodes

My mom does this too, but I'm not sure if she's even looking at the tv. She just like zones out.

Mastermind

My mother could be the most insufferable woman in the world when she wanted to. She stood in the middle of my entryway, wearing a one-piece bathing suit, a sheer cover-up that hung like an oversize t-shirt on her slight frame, and sandals with heels taller than any of the shoes in my closet. "I can't believe that you're going to work today. You're more interested in your company loyalty than spending time with your mother."

I had so many things that I could say, tell her that the house we stood in was part of my company loyalty, that the pool she was going to lounge at was part of my company loyalty, the food that she expected when she returned was part of my company loyalty. Instead I nodded at her and took the shortest path out of the conversation, "I will only be gone for a few hours." I grabbed her sun hat from one of the hooks on the wall and handed it to her.

Snatching it away from me, she turned for the door. She huffed through her nose and started to collect her things from the console table into her oversized, wicker-style bag.

Happy that she was ignoring me again, I checked myself over in the mirror behind the door. The jeans were so ugly. I could almost understand her all-consuming disappointment in me from the jeans alone. They were an ugly, bright blue, like they'd never been worn before. I was almost convinced that the Edenbriar Laundry Service redyed the jeans each wash. There was one time, when I'd first moved in with Kimberly, that we'd written down the number on the inside of each item of clothing before dropping them into the shute, just to make sure that we really did get the same clothes back as we sent in. When we checked, the item numbers matched, but there was a part of me that was still convinced that they did something to them. Kimberly had whispered to me late at night that maybe they manufactured a new pair of jeans and assigned the same number to them every time. I always laugh the thought away, but it always comes back.

I ran my hands down the front of my black t-shirt, smoothing out the nonexistent wrinkles. I grabbed the door handle, plastered on my smile, and greeted the outdoors.

My mother pushed past me out the door first, putting her sunglasses on to shield her from the sun. "I will see you later. Tonight, we'll go to the outlet shops to buy some things to take home with me." She made a shooing motion, showing off the premium manicure that she'd gotten the day before. "Go on, prove to your employer that they're more important to you than I am."

My fingernails dug into my palms, and I pressed my lips together. That employer is the only reason that she could go to the outlet shops in the first place. I stood in the door frame taking deep breaths, watching as my mom sauntered down the sidewalk in the direction of the pool facility.

Kimberly said that I had more of a temper than I used to, that she was looking forward to the day that I put my mother in her place, but I wasn't. I was going to bite my tongue off before I did that. It was a wonder that my mom came to visit at all, since she never thought anything I did was worthwhile.

I closed my door behind me. The automatic lock turned closed, and its usual chime let me know that the security system had run a quick check of the doors and windows, finding everything secure. I walked to the bus stop, waited with three other people wearing the same ugly jeans and the same closed-off look, then boarded the next bus to the center.

The bus let us off in the carport dome; various share cars were dropping people off from the neighborhoods beyond the center's suburbs. The idea of the dress code was to make us all feel the same, be the same, but we weren't, and clothes didn't disguise the differences. The people from the suburbs had blank faces, rode in buses full of people but didn't speak a single word. The people from the neighborhoods beyond had darker circles under their eyes, but they smiled kindly to each other and chatted as they walked into the center.

In the crowd of morning shift workers, I found Bea and Kim, standing off to the side, waiting for me. Bea was on her glastic tablet, flicking through whatever content she'd subscribed to on the center's server.

I didn't even own a phone; it just didn't seem like it was necessary in Edenbriar. My mom complained to me about it at every chance she got, but considering the public kiosks, our work tablets, and our home installations, I was able to access my messages wherever I was. It was hard to take and make phone calls, sure, but I wanted all of my calls to be neatly scheduled so I could prepare for them anyway.

"Gogo!" Kim waved enthusiastically, welcoming me to work. "So, how's your mom?" Her sarcasm was clear.

We waded into the stream of people entering the building. We waited for Bea to finish and place her phone into a locker. "Well, she's my mom." I shrugged.

I wished Kim could be there, holding my hand through it, but that just wasn't the kind of life I was allowed to live. When my mom was there, Kimberly had to be elsewhere, and this time, elsewhere was at Bea's house, crashing in her spare room.

Kimberly grabbed my hand and swung it. We followed Bea through the double doors, and into the queue at the check-in desk. The room was designed to make you feel awake. It buzzed with bright yellows and lively oranges on the walls, the LED lights seemed to multiply with every blink.

"Dodge comma Beatrice." Bea told the check-in unit. The input processed for a second before the unit thanked her for checking in that morning and handed her a work tablet with her assignment list and headset, and name tag.

"Yang comma Kimberly." She hadn't let go of my hand, forcing me to bear witness to her usual morning ruse.

The check-in unit processed for a second. "Yang, Kimberly is not on the daily roster. If there is an error, I can direct you to the nearest HR node for further processing."

Kim squeezed my hand. "Damn, I could've sworn that was my name. Hey, Gogo, have you heard about this?"

She smiled warmly, looking over my face, taking in the exasperated expression that I wore every time she did this. "Oh well, someone should really get on that. Check in Trent comma Kimberly." The processor checked her in.

"Yang comma Margo." I checked in, receiving the usual daily welcome package.

We clipped on our name tags and compared assignments for the day. Bea was supposed to work in the server room, one of the most depressing shift positions you could pull, especially since the monitoring system's latest updates. A few weeks earlier, a node had tried to self-disconnect, requiring firewall updates and making our jobs that much harder.

Kim was going to be a tour guide, which would be a highly-prized, easy shift if she didn't pull them constantly. Something about Kim made her perfect for tours. She had long straight hair that fell perfectly down her back, never frizzing or carrying the smell of the smoke. Her round face made the headset look cute instead of dorky. And, on top of it all, her intonation and welcoming gestures really shined during the tours. She'd once given me a mock tour of our home, trying to prove how shit she was at it, but she was actually really good. She groaned and peeked at my task list.

"Hey, you'll be coding today. So cool." She pointed at my tablet. "And we have the same lunch break. Yeah, lunchtime date in the cafeteria," she gloated, pumping a fist at her side.

Bea frowned, "I'm on an early lunch, then I'm assigned to the chat team." She put the tablet in her back pocket. "I guess, I'll see you after work." She unfolded her headset and slid it onto her face, aligning the sensors at her temples and resting the screen piece on the bridge of her nose. The spectacle screens flashed white as they connected to the system, then Bea turned on her heel and marched away toward the server room.

While the check-in thing was definitely Kim's routine, the next part was our routine. We always held hands and told each other that we'd see each other soon, before putting on our headsets. Kim offered a huge grin and one-handedly tucked the spectacles onto her face, then her other hand went slack in mine. She stayed though, watching intently, until I put my headset on, too.

I couldn't be sure what other people felt when they put the headsets on, but I was sure that we didn't all feel the same. The discussion boards on the associate portal were full of theories. Not all of them were worth reading, but there were a few that seemed plausible.

One theory posited that when, how, and how often you've processed are the key factors, and that your first experience had a huge impact on the rest of your processing career. If your first processing was under stress or duress, then the system took note of your high levels of adrenaline and fear, logging it in your forever record. Every time you processed, the system logged your mood levels and other activity, prorating the data points to decide how to regulate the system node. These metrics, once skewed, couldn't be unskewed.

Another theory pointed the finger at suburban schools and their technology curriculum. Students that attend the schools in a center's suburbs would usually receive a technical education focused on the node dynamic, teaching children different safety techniques and procedures for processing and interacting with units. They cited that children in the suburban tech program usually got to practice in a classroom environment, with a facilitator guiding them, which made them better adept at it.

The third theory was the one that I thought about the most. People thought differently, so people processed differently. When I reread the posts under the forum thread, Kim would shake her head at me and tell me that it's the dumbest theory she'd ever heard. I disagreed. The theory was simple, sure, but highly complex, and most associates didn't know what to make of it, evidenced by the sheer number of reactions on the post but lack of responses. The original post included links to a psychological study on trauma, a sociological study on interconnectedness, and an engineering article on system emergence. It all came together to paint a vivid picture, traumatic even.

The center's coding room was on one of the corporate levels, where the building looked more like an office building than a warehouse. There were workstations lined up across the level with desktop touch screen and ergonomic chairs. There was a smattering of people seated there, but that didn't mean we were working together or knew each other. We physically sat next to each other, but were virtually isolated.

Sitting at my coding station, my headset buzzed hard at at my temples, taking me into my workspace. A part of my mind settled into its usual cubbyhole in the associate portal, skimming through my bookmarks for any new takes on the theories, looping through my lengthy list of highly specific search terms to see if there were new threads. But, most of my mind dug through M code in our local sandbox.

I was really good at coding, so it had become like touring had become for Kim, a regular tasking. I was often in the sandbox with three other minds, fiddling and fixing code that sectors of nodes had cobbled together from help desk tickets, dictionaries, and search algorithms. Perfecting something that was disjoint and broken into a machine.

Today was different, though, because I was the only person in the sandbox. In the relative privacy, I had to admit that it was so much better that way. I didn't have to fix their mistakes or chase them away from the part I was working on, didn't have to explain to the others what the piece of code was obviously meant to do.

As I finished with the bulk of the code, I pulled my mind away from the script, looking at the whole of it. It was still a bit sloppy. I needed to rename some of the variables and parameters now that I understood what they were used for in the end, and I would have to add some comments throughout the code to make sure that the more complex processes were documented. But the code compiled, and that's what mattered.

Knowing in some core way that it was lunch time, I pulled myself back further, out of the scripting file, out of the sandbox, out and out, until I was pulling in. Pulling myself into the associate portal, a pinging sound became incessant. The tone was all encompassing, coming from the messages application on the portal's homepage.

I had twenty-six missed messages and three missed calls. The red notification icons hurt in a specifically hard-to-ignore color. In the app, I had a number of unread communications; most were from my mother. I skimmed through them, getting the gist of it from the one-line previews. My mom's visitor ID wasn't working on the Edenbriar amenities, and she was pissed about it.

The latest messages were mostly capital letters and included phrases like 'second class citizen' and 'absolutely unacceptable'. The earlier the message, the more passive the aggressive became. Then the earliest message, which was from the processing center's network administration address, scrolled into my mind's eye. "Congratulations on your promotion," it said with a red and orange confetti banner, "Please proceed to an administration node to complete your formwork."

―●―

"You missed our lunch break date." Kim pouted, leaning against the sleek, cement wall of the processing center in the carport dome. "You better have a good reason." She was upset of course, but not as upset as she would have been if I hadn't messaged her that I wasn't going to be able to make it to the cafeteria for lunch that day.

I hoped my news was good enough for her to forgive me. "I've been promoted?" I hadn't meant to say it like a question, but it definitely sounded like one.

She pushed off the wall. "Really?" She grabbed both of my hands and bounced on the balls of her feet. "That's amazing! I'm so proud of you!" She looked so genuinely happy for me that it made me feel a little bit better about the whole thing.

Bea gave a short, impressed nod, the edges of her mouth were turned down and she raised her eyebrows. "So what are you promoted to?"

"Well, I'm not in the rotational pool anymore. I'll be coding full time." I pointed to my name tag, which had been swapped out to say MR Margaret Yang and smiled, happy that my friends were being supportive.

Kim's hand squeezed mine. "You're so smart, Gogo. I just wanna smother you with kisses and go out to celebrate!" In the logical next response, her shoulders fell slack and her head lolled as she groaned. "I can't believe this happened when your mom is here."

Nodding along, Bea shrugged. "Yeah, we'll have to wait to do the celebrating after she leaves." She took her glastic phone from her pocket, unlocked it with face recognition, and started to scroll the company feed. "At least it'll show your mom that you're good at your work."

I cringed at the mention of my mother. "She is less than impressed."

"What? Why?" Kim swung our hands out and in with her exclamations. "You've literally proven to Alps that you're smart enough to be a full-time coder." She rocked back, sizing me up, looking me over in a way that made me both unbearably nervous and unbearably warm. "My Gogo is a Master Coder." She raised and lowered her eyebrow at me suggestively.

Feeling my cheeks flush, I squeezed Kim's hand but turned to address Bea. "I was in the coding sandbox and missed the notification when it came in, so her visitor pass wouldn't work." I turned my eyes to the pavement. "She was pissed."

Despite the very real dread that I was feeling, its jagged edge was smoothed over by the sound of my friends snickering. I huffed out a breath and rolled my eyes, peeking up to look at them.

Bea was masking her laughter much better than Kim, but Bea was always better at hiding that sort of thing. Kim's face was turning red from the effort to hold it in.

I cracked a small smile back at them. "She was stuck in the pool building's vestibule."

"Oh my god!" Kim blurted out, laughing to the point of tears. "That's even funnier than what I was thinking."

Bea pinched at the bridge of her nose, sniffing in deep to catch her breath. "I can't think of a worse place. I know she's pissed and all, but it's almost like Alps hates her, too."

I missed Kim already. When I got home, my mom had packed her bags and moved them into the entryway. I couldn't say I was surprised. Honestly, I mostly felt relief that she was going to be leaving, that Kim would be able to come back home soon.

Like I usually did, I ducked through the kitchen to the laundry room. I peeled the ugly jeans off and deposited them into the shute, replacing them with a pair of sleep-soft shorts from the clean laundry.

"Margo, is that you?"

I wasn't sure who else she thought it could be. "Yeah, it's me," I called. I picked up the basket of clean clothes from the laundry lift and pressed the button to send the little elevator pod back to the central laundry. "I'm back from work." I turned out of the laundry room and into the kitchen.

My mother stood in the middle of the kitchen in a sundress and and a different pair of platform sandals. Her mouth screwed around a few times as she looked at me. I wasn't sure what to make of her like this. With her luggage in the entryway, I'd expected to find her in one of her brightly colored jumpsuits with a scarf tied around her hair ready to travel home. In my work t-shirt and pajama shorts, I felt underdressed in my own kitchen.

"Is something wrong?" Her silence was worse than her nagging. I shifted the laundry basket on my hip.

She narrowed her eyes at me. "I don't feel welcome here." And as soon as the first words came out of her mouth, she just kept going. "I don't feel safe. What if I get stuck on a transport and you can't find me?"

Impossible. She'd message me, obviously.

"What if I try to get my prescriptions and I'm denied?"

She gets her prescriptions, written by my big pharma brother, by mail drone to her phone's location every week.

"What if there's a smoke warning and I get stuck outside?"

While that was technically possible, Edenbriar, along with the other inner suburbs, had invested in carbon capture technology way back when the smoke was barely a health risk. From Edenbriar, it was hard to believe that the smoke was so bad unless you were busing through it into the center.

She folded her arms across herself and stared unseeingly at the laundry basket under my arm. "Who's Kimberly?"

I blinked at her. "Who's who exactly?" My arms felt like ice.

My mother wasn't a patient woman. "Kimberly," her voice was loud. "When I was stuck in that lobby today, a security unit came to help. They asked if I had tried to contact you, which I had, then they asked if I had tried to contact Kimberly Trent. When I asked who that was, they said that Kimberly Trent is the emergency contact on file for your employee number."

"Oh, Kimberly. She's a friend from work." I hiked the laundry basket up on my hip.

My mother stared at me, expression mad but in a blank way that I couldn't read further.

Past me would have waited calmly and blankly myself, waited until my mother inevitably caved to her own emotion. But I wasn't past me. "Actually, she's more than a friend from work; she's my girlfriend." I swallowed hard. "Kimberly is my girlfriend, my live-with girlfriend, and if she had it her way, we'd be fiances or married by now." I gripped the laundry basket tight. "She's beautiful and loud and bubbly, and I love her." I stomped my opposite foot. I wouldn't curse in front of my mother, but that stomp had 'fuck you' written all over it.

My mother was still blank-mad. Her expression broke open, and she made a guttural sound. She strode across the room, leaving the kitchen, on her way to leaving my house. "I don't care that you're gay. Be gay!"

I shoved the laundry basket onto the kitchen counter and followed her, not feeling as ashamed of my outburst as I expected to. I should've stayed quiet, but I couldn't after all that I said. "I will be gay!" I yelled after her.

She spun around, her sundress fluttering. "That's fine!" She yelled back. She tapped the handle for her largest suitcase; it shot up, telescoping up for her to use to guide it along beside her. She furiously snatched up her second suitcase, and put the strap over her shoulder.

"Then what are you mad about?" I knew my face was messed up. I could feel the grimace, the way my nostril twitched.

"You-" She struggled with dramatically turning to me again with the awkward weight of her luggage strapped to her body. She had to take baby steps to turn back to me.

"Me?" I raised an eyebrow, sunk into my hip, and added sarcastically, "Why didn't you say so?"

She huffed. "You have no respect for me." Her stare was intense, and it forced me to swallow my sarcasm. "You ignore me when I come to visit; you go off to work and leave me to wander around here all day. You don't take my calls or messages when I need your help. You don't have me listed as an emergency contact." She took a breath, then her eyebrows pinched together in the center of her face. "And you didn't even tell me that you're gay."

Technically I did, literally moments before, but my mouth would not move. My mother had frozen my jaw shut with the ice in her words. I could only stare.

"Your brother booked me for the night at one of the resort buildings." She teetered as she reached for her sunhat still on the hook.

I opened my mouth to say something back, but I couldn't think of what to say. I didn't even feel all that angry at her, just happy that she was leaving, content that we'd argued out loud for the first time since I'd completed my secondary education track. I gently lifted her sunhat from the hook and passed it to her.

She took it.

This was usually the part of the trip when I lied to her, telling her that I was glad that she visited, that I looked forward to her coming to visit again, that she should call when she got home. But after what was said, it seemed like the wrong send-off.

Her face pinched together in frustration, almost regretful frustration. She didn't look at me, making her baby steps to turn back to the door. "I'm sure Kimberly is lovely." It was curt, but it was almost civil.

"She is." I agreed.

My mother grabbed the door handle and let herself out. "Congratulations on your promotion." It was equally curt. She shut the door behind her.

I sighed, still mostly relief. "Thanks," I replied to the empty room.

IN NEWS AND UPCOMING EVENTS

Siblings Awarded Scholarship and Education Award in Same Year

Written by Kellem Hall, Independent Reporter
Reviewed by Jaxon Treau, Alps News and Blogs
Posted 2810 days ago, Last Edited 2807 days ago

In a turn of events that surprised everyone in Greater Greenville, two siblings were awarded the Corporate Council Higher Education Award and the Greenville Processing Center's Education Hub Scholarship.

Mildred and Ruthie Dodge were born five years apart in the Outer Banks. If you ask anyone from their social circles, they'll tell you they knew the two girls were destined for greatness. Their mother and father weren't available to meet with me, but long-time neighbors, Francis and Sati Mulberry were available for a what was supposed to be a brief chat.

Francis, who had retired from teaching, watched the awardees and their other siblings when their parents took concurrent shifts at the center. She waxed nostalgic as we discussed the girls, "Mildred had a knack for questions. As soon as you finished answering one question, she'd have another one ready for you. Good questions, one after another." Francis went on to chronicle some of the conundrums that Mildred would think her way into and then out of. "She was always thinking bigger than herself, bigger than all of us. Needless to say," Francis continued, "I'm not surprised that she won the award. The Corporate Council needs smart girls like her."

Sati, Francis' wife, brought snacks for us to share as we continued our conversation about the awardees. "Ruthie was always getting into trouble," Francis added, "but it was the kind of righteous trouble that you [read about in historical accounts](). She didn't just want to understand something like her sister did. She wanted to get inside it, touch all the pieces." Sati smiled fondly as she recalled when Ruthie had removed a panel from a pod they were travelling in. "Pods were so small – this was before the eight-seater model. Francis took Mildred and the younger siblings in the first pod, and Ruthie, Bea, and I waited for the second one. I forget what we were out for." Francis: "Errands? A movie?" Sati: "Don't know, but I dozed off in the pod on the way back." Francis jumped back in, "She didn't wake up until the pod stopped, and Ruthie had disassembled and untangled half of the pod's control board wiring." They laughed and Sati put another biscuit on my plate.

The Mulberrys don't have children of their own, but act like another set of grandparents for many families in their community, including the Dodge family next door. This kind of neighborly relationship is more common in the rural areas, where people travel further to work and learn. When I asked them what they hoped the Dodge sisters would get from the article if they read it, Sati smiled softly, "They shouldn't need to be reminded, but we are so proud of them both."

Goldfish

I schooled my face into something becoming of the NationAlive CEO's eldest son. I swallowed the lump that had formed in my throat and waited as the call rang through to my father's office. The projection bubble, a spherical display emanating from the projector embedded in my school desk, was labeled with my father's name, growing and shrinking with each ring.

When I was still little, before I started at the academy, my older sister had told me that my call anxiety was silly and that I needed to stifle it if I wanted to be anything worthwhile. It hadn't been easy, but my therapist had recommended I breathe in time with the bubble's slow pulses on the display. The trick worked really well for me, and my parents almost canceled my therapy entirely, since they figured that I must've been fixed.

I no longer saw that therapist. When NationAlive came out with their all-in-one artificial intelligence healthcare system, my coverage denied my need to see a therapist and my parents wouldn't pay for something that wasn't required. Only the best, most cutting-edge products would serve us, according to my father. We use the same products as the employees to show that we believe in them, according to my mother. When we'd first swapped over, I'd asked the AI to schedule me with my therapist, but it only assured me that my health history didn't require me to see one and that I could talk to it if I needd help, which really wasn't the same.

The line connected and my father's assistant appeared on the screen. "Ah, Hulk, how can I help you?" The young men that served as my father's assistants all had the same look to them, sharp-eyed and bored. They also all seemed to have long dark hair, high cheekbones, and thick lips, but my sister had warned me to never bring it up, so I didn't.

I didn't know this assistant's name. "Hi, I wanted to check to see if my father would be attending today's awards rally." I couldn't look him in the eyes even through a display, so I stared through the projection to a photo digitally tacked to my desk screen.

The assistant pursed his lips, eyes flicking through his own displays.

Thinking back, I couldn't remember if my father had attended Demeter's awards rally, but I hadn't been paying a lot of attention. Demeter was eight years older than me, so I had still been in primary grades when she was graduating. I knew that my father had kept her academy tie and displayed it in a trophy case in his home office along with her official graduation picture and a few digital clippings of different articles that featured her.

"Hmmm." The assistant's face pinched further, but he didn't say anything.

I cleared my throat to relieve the tightening lump there, earning a quick glare.

"It's not on his calendar." The assistant responded, his glaring softening around the edges. "When is the rally? I can add a reminder."

I considered backing out of the call with some flimsy excuse, but a voice in my head that sounded suspiciously like Demeter reminded me that I shouldn't expect something if I didn't ask for it. I focused my gaze back on the assistant, just between his eyebrows, where a shiny, dermal implant caught the light like a third eye. "It's this afternoon at second hour. I had forwarded the flyer when it was-"

"Ah, yes, I see it." The assistant's eyes were flicking around again, probably sifting through different message inboxes. "This afternoon is an important meeting between NationAlive and Alps Landscape, so he won't be able to make it."

While I hadn't really expected that he'd attend, I at least figured that he'd tune in from a pod or an office somewhere, maybe send a synchronous message of congratulations after the final results debuted. I gripped my knees under my desk. "Ah, I see." A smile would look sad, so I sucked my lips against my teeth.

"I'm sorry, Hulk." He ended the call.

I got to the auditorium early because it felt like wallowing to wait around in my dorm any longer. I claimed my and my best friend's usual seats up high in the bleachers, right where the dome above met the seating pit below. The end-of-year awards rally had the student population of Breaux Academy buzzing. Even students who were notoriously late were arriving early. Everyone filing in talked animatedly, and most of them wore their uniforms in an unusual state of disarray. Though school was still in session for two more weeks, most student examinations were complete and the teaching staff had given up on uniform inspections. As long as you came in wearing something from the uniform catalog that covered the most important areas of you body, it didn't matter how you wore it.

From the seats at the top, I could see everything happening in the pit. That was the reason why we sat up here, to people-watch. I couldn't stop myself from watching the section of the pit that had been cordoned off for visitors. Most of Breaux Academy's rallies were live-streamed, available for student families and the city's general population, but very few allowed in-person guests.

In the visitor section, I found people who were fascinatingly boring in an all too familiar way. They wore expensive shimmer tech and pearlescent suits that caught the dome's light in weird ways that the old-style, recycled-fiber uniforms didn't. I squinted and turned away, intent on watching the students come in instead.

When Fennel walked through the doors, I waved at them, indicating the empty seat next to me. They said something to their classmates before making a buzzer-route toward me. They took the bleacher steps two at a time and slid in next to me naturally. "So," they tugged lightly at the end of my tie, "you're still actually wearing it?"

Their tie was tied around their bare calf. When I looked at it, they propped their foot on the back of the stadium chair in front of them, showing it off. "You like?"

I shook my head. "You should wear it right. It'll get ruined tied like that." I adjusted the knot in my tie.

"It's the last two weeks that we ever have to wear them." They dropped their foot down, startling some younger students finding seats a few rows ahead of us. "I might as well have some fun with it." They flicked at my tie. "You could too."

Batting their hand away, I rolled my eyes.

Fennel's grin faltered for a moment as their eyes dragged over the tie. "We're almost done." They resettled themself in the seat, tucking their skort down in the back.

I knew that Fennel had an entirely different view on this place, that they had a deep desire to get out of here and into the real world. We talked about it whenever we seemed to be by ourselves, like really by ourselves, like that one time we ate edibles in one of the rec center's private karaoke rooms.

They pulled their feet up onto their seat and hugged their knees. "I can't wait to get out of here, move back to the mainland, do my apprenticeship with the corporate council, and start making a difference." They squeezed their knees harder, staring at the back of the seat in front of them, gazing into a future they were trying so hard to manifest.

While I completely understood why they felt that way and knew it was selfish of me to think otherwise, I really couldn't bring myself to look forward to what came after the academy. The fate that awaited me was moving back to my father's house and interning with one of the subsidiaries. I still hadn't opened the asynchronous message from the recruiter. I knew pushing it off was a bad idea, but finals had been a perfect excuse.

I carefully placed my hand on their shoulder and squeezed. I took in a deep breath then let it out, squeezing my hand on their shoulder again in time with it. I racked my brain for something worthwhile to say.

The lights in the auditorium dimmed, saving me from a response, and music blasted out from the surround speakers hanging from the ceiling in a circle. "Make some noise!" The pep rally host was Brigette Kline, our student body president and the eldest daughter of one of the top macro implant moguls. She had long, platinum-colored hair that matched the color of her metal implants along her brow ridge, filling in where the second half of each eyebrow would be. She grinned as the opening music repeated itself but louder. "I can't hear you over the music. You really need to make some noise!"

Fennel and I screamed, breaking the tension that had settled across us. Their legs fell from their grip; I felt their shoes slam into the stadium flooring, but couldn't hear the thud over the roar of the crowd. They smiled at me, and I smiled back, worries about our futures drowned out for now. I slid my hand across their shoulders and squeezed us together in an excited half-hug.

We settled in together, watching the event below commence. If this rally was anything like the awards rallies from previous years, it would be a spectacle, showing off the best of Breaux Academy and its students.

The marching band played the corporate council's jingle and our school's anthem first, then the cheer squad joined them on the court to perform some of their most popular routines. Someone came out in the Breaux Bear Mascot costume, hyping up the students for the cheer squad's big finale.

Next, like most rallies, the robotics and visualizations teams displayed their handiwork by entertaining the crowd and tens of thousands of viewers with a drone and hologram display. This time, they rendered a short sequence of our mascot exploring and navigating through a series of themed rooms until the holographic visual shrunk and landed on the floor. Then, the physical mascot and the hologram mascot performed a choreographed final duel. Eventually, the physical mascot won, standing over the hologram version, laid out on the auditorium floor, defeated. A large hologram sword glowed, appearing in the air above them; the physical mascot took it and situated it in their hand.

"And now," Brigette's voice microphone gave a loud squeal of feedback over the sound system. The audience winced, and there was an obvious muting, adjusting, and unmuting. "And now," she repeated over the looping music from the duel's conclusion, voice wobbly from something like embarrassment. "Breaux Academy of Arts and Technology presents this academic year's results!"

The physical mascot on stage plunged the sword into its doppelganger, and the hologram exploded outward, washing everyone with a flash of light. Following the explosion, the auditorium's main lights dimmed further, and the drones scattered to their usual places, equidistant around the dome, projector displays throwing light inward toward the floor. The entire space washed blue, and waves of soft aqua light rippled through the room.

Only Brigette remained on the clearing at the base of the seating pit, standing in the middle, illuminated by a barely discernible spotlight of lighter blue. "Our school," she waved a hand through the air. On cue, holographic bubbles rose from the floor, and when they cleared, fish filled the room. One fish for each student at Breaux Academy, each varying shades of blue to green to yellow to orange to gold.

In contrast to the rest of the event, the screams and excited shouts had vanished, replaced by the hushed wonder that the display always inspired. It was like the feeling you got when you visited the New New Orleans Underdome, the public recreational park under the city center, where you could watch the fish and submerged passenger crafts go by. It was like the feeling you got when you went on the mandatory class trip to the sea wall, looking at the abandoned city structures that used to be the Big Easy, completely submerged.

Even though it all must've been rehearsed, especially given the stunning choreography of the fight sequence, Brigette still had to shake herself away from the heft of the display. She cleared her throat, "Our students with academic distinction." Most of the fish swimming around the room faded out, almost transparent, leaving a number of high fish still visible, almost glowing with their bright orange and gold scales. Soft yellow lights appeared in the stands, illuminating the corresponding soon-to-be graduates.

Having recovered, the student body whistled and clapped for them.

Because I was curious, I glanced to the guest section, but I couldn't see their faces well enough to gauge their interest. They're heads were tilted up; each one cocked at the same angle, looking to the very center at the top of the dome. A part of me was disappointed; they were interested in nothing but the best. I vaguely wondered if my dad would do the same, but of course he would. When the yellow spotlights faded, so did the applause.

"Our students with great academic distinction."

Another, smaller set of fish were highlighted, and another, smaller set of students were spotlighted, this set included me. I wasn't a star student, and I procrastinated far longer than my sister or father liked. In fact, I had been much more interested in my writing and art than school, but when your best friend's favorite hobbies were studying and having deep conversations about the future, you were bound to be a bit more studious.

Fennel shifted awkwardly in their seat as they clapped for the honorees. They were nervous for their results.

Which was absolutely ludicrous. Fennel was one of the smartest students in our year, perhaps *the* smartest. They had a lot riding on their grades, so they'd always studied extra hard. They were a scholarship student, so they weren't there to fuck around, unlike half of the elite students. I grimaced down at the nearly invisible blue fish at the bottom of the display, directing my gaze at the ones big enough to be rising fifth years. Most of their parents would get them into an early-level internship over the summer that would bump their status up, just like me. I grimaced harder.

Vibrating with anxiety, Fennel bit one of their blue-painted fingernails. It was almost laughable that they were anxious, but if I laughed, it would definitely be taken the wrong way, so I pressed my lips together into an unmoving line. By process of elimination, they had to be in the last category; there was absolutely no way they'd been awarded no academic distinction. I caught their gaze, trying to ask what they needed without saying anything aloud.

Just like when we'd first hugged in the library before our freshman year philosophy final, just like when we had held hands on the sea wall field trip as sophomores, just like when we'd snuck off with my dad's boat after our junior year dance, something unsaid passed between us, and I felt absolutely obligated to hold them. I shifted forward and wrapped both arms around their shoulders, pulling until their right elbow was situated almost painfully in my gut; I tucked my chin down so my forehead rested on the rumpled collar of their oxford shirt.

Fennel's fingers grabbed at my blazer, hugging my arm to them like they would a safety-issued life jacket. They breathed heavily a few times trying to calm their erratic nerves, before they settled into the embrace.

The intensity of our friendship always scared me. The underlying feeling that this was quite possibly more than friendship scared me so much more.

Through the stiff air around us, I heard Brigette announce, "Our students with the highest academic distinction." I couldn't see the fish from where I'd buried myself in Fennel's neck, but I could see the glow that surrounded us in the stadium seating. They jolted, tapping violently at my elbow. I retreated enough to see their ecstatic expression, splitting into a matching grin for them, then we had another unsaid moment, then we hugged again.

•—•

"I can't believe it!" We'd left as soon as the rally had ended. Unlike many of our classmates, our glastic tablets weren't buzzing or ringing or flashing with congratulatory messages. It was easy to step over and around everyone, making it out the door in record time.

Outside the auditorium doors, the air felt less stuffy, probably because the hallways hadn't been packed full of tiny drones, casting heat and light across manufactured fog. Fennel spread their arms out to their sides, sniffing in a big breath like we were topside. "I just can't believe it!"

I sighed at them. "I'm not sure why? It was obvious that you were the top of the class for at least the last four and a half years."

They narrowed their eyes at me. "Nothing here is that simple. I kept expecting some paywall to be thrown up in front of me or some recommendation requirement or some other bullshit."

"Woah, language." I shushed them, pointedly not looking toward the security sensors spaced out along the ceiling and adjusting my tie.

They turned around, walking backward and grinning at me. "I can't give a fuck anymore." They laughed, and the relief in that laugh settled into me too.

"Hulk Devros?"

Fennel's open grin shut off immediately, and they leveled a stony gaze over my shoulder toward the voice.

I turned around to see someone following up behind us.

Students were leaving the auditorium now, milling about on their way back to their rooms. They definitely weren't a student, wearing a transparent, oversized suit jacket over a pearly colored sleeveless, turtle-necked bodysuit. They held out a card to me. "Nilla Watkins, she/her. I recruit for MIDAS Tech."

Taking the card, I held it pinched in both hands in front of me, awkwardly. I looked it over. It told me nothing more than she'd already said, just in a curly, almost-illegible script accompanied by a crown-like logo. Out in public, if someone called my name, I was supposed to turn the other direction and alert someone on my family's security team. Stranger danger and all that.

But, I glanced at the bright, orange visitor pass stuck to her jacket. She had to check in to be here, and MIDAS Tech was the subsidiary that I was expected to intern with next year. And, I was twenty years old in one of the most highly-secured schools in the world. "Hello, Ms. Watkins. How can I help you?"

Fennel inched up next to me and tapped my arm. "Hey, Hulk, I'm going to head up to my room." They looked over my face, but I didn't meet their eyes. "Okay then, see you later."

"See you," I responded, still looking directly at the visitor, who was almost smirking? There was a pleasant, default smile on her face, but one corner of it quirked down. She watched Fennel walk away.

Ms. Watkins' turned her attention back to me. "At a meeting recently, your sister and I got a chance to sit down and discuss your CV."

There were even more students in the hallway. They gave us as wide of a berth as they could, but not without openly staring at Ms. Watkins. She seemed to be the only visitor who had exited the auditorium in this direction, so she stuck out spectacularly. I briefly wondered if I should invite her somewhere more private, but I still didn't entirely trust her story. I tucked her card into my pocket. "My sister discussed my CV with you?"

"Well," she took an exaggerated breath, "I hadn't gotten any response from you, so I made do with the resources I had."

I think the part of her story that was hardest to believe was that she was a recruiter. She seemed too posh; the recruiters that I'd met at career events and on tours of various regional offices always seemed frazzled, jumpy, overworked. Ms. Watkins looked like she'd just stepped out of a classic, petrol car for her first day on a luxury holiday.

"I have been focused on my exams and had expected to catch up on my messages in the next few days." I turned my expression down, in the same practiced way my sister showed polite, apologetic concern. "I supposed that's no help to you now though." I shifted my shoulders, that business shrug that my father made when he was moving on from a topic that was beneath him. "I'm sure my sister was able to provide you with everything you need." It was a sentence, but it was a question.

She didn't answer. The other students had mostly dispersed by now, only a few stragglers typing on their phones. She looked me up and down, effectively pinning me in place. Assessing me, she walked a circle around me, like the 3-D scan captures. "Yes, she was able to complete the paperwork." Her glossy, white flats didn't make any sound as she walked around me, but I could track the swishing of her bodysuit's flared legs. When she finished her turnabout, she didn't turn back to me, instead standing in front of me looking to the side. She was extremely thin, the kind of thin that was only possible if you consumed IVs instead of solids. "I prefer to meet candidates before I offer them internships. I expect them to complete an interview process."

She was trying to make me nervous, and I was, but I had years of experience with this kind of thing. Even Fennel admitted that interviewing was my top skill, as long as it wasn't over a call line.

Ms. Watkins cocked her head and looked me over again. She pursed her lips, making a decision. "We were running out of opportunities to meet." She turned away, poised to leave. "Your sister assured me that you would meet expectations, but I still needed to see for myself."

I cleared my throat. "You're not a recruiter," I said.

She didn't look back, but she nodded, swaying her large, pink earrings. "Your sister didn't wait to call that out, when I met with her. You have more tact than she does. That's good. It'll make you more marketable."

When she turned back around, she was smiling. It was a real smile, but it was still cool. She pulled another business card from one of her bodysuit's pockets and handed it to me. "I wasn't lying. I do recruit for MIDAS Tech, and I have been trying to reach you."

I didn't look at the card, pushing it into my pocket with the other one.

This time, when she turned, there was more energy in her step. "Think of me as your top investor."

Without thinking, I went straight to Fennel's room. When they opened the door, they had their eyebrows raised so high that their forehead wrinkled. They had changed out of their school uniform into a gray tracksuit. "So what was that about?" They waved me in.

Breaux Academy's dorms were standardized. Everyone had their own suite; each had an attached bathroom and came with a dresser, a multi-use desk, and a bed. We didn't have dorm inspections except at the beginning and end of each year, so some students would swap out their furniture, sending it to storage. I didn't, and Fennel didn't. It just didn't seem worth the hassle or cost.

I sat on their desk chair and they sat on the bed. "She was from MIDAS Tech."

"Yeah, I was there for that part. She was a recruiter from MIDAS Tech."

"She wasn't," I insisted. I pulled the second card from my pants pocket. It was a sturdy card, made of thick plastic.

Fennel looked alarmed. "She lied?"

"No..." I handed the card to Fennel. "She's Head of Personnel Investments."

Fennel's nose scrunched up, taking the card. "You mean personal investments?"

I just shook my head while they read the card. "Oh." They flipped it over. "This is an RFID card. There's probably more about her." They pointed to the scan logo in the bottom corner of the back of the card. Fennel didn't wait for me to agree. They rolled me out of their way and placed the card on their desk.

Three windows opened on the display screen. One was a browser window showing Nilla Watkin's professional portfolio in the Corporate Council's database; another opened the About page from MIDAS Tech's website. The last window was a file explorer containing three files. One was labeled READ ME.txt, one was labeled RUN1.exe, and the last was labeled RUN2.exe.

Sat on the very edge of their bed, Fennel turned their body toward the display screen. They dragged the Corporate Council window closer to their side to read. I tapped open the READ ME file.

Mr. Devros,

Thank you for meeting with me today. It was exciting to meet you in-person after studying your CV and files for so long. I'm pleased to inform you that you've been selected for a paid internship at MIDAS Tech in the Executive Suite. As you know, MIDAS Tech researches and develops modeling and printing solutions for the commons. I think your project experience and skillset will serve you and the XCOM members you'll work with.

To accept your internship with us, run the two programs attached. One will access your school's records; the other will send your records and acceptance message to the proper personnel here at MIDAS.

The deadline for acceptance is COB today. It's unfortunate that we weren't able to schedule this interview earlier in the month.

Looking forward to working with you,
Nilla Watkins
Head of Personnel Investment

Fennel had finished with the browser window and was leaning over to read the note from Ms. Watkins. They were close enough that I could see the freckles under their eyes. They were hard to see from further away since the coppery color of the freckles blended with their red-brown complexion. Their nose crinkled. On their side of the screen, they opened a sandbox from the start menu and dragged the file explorer window into it.

"What's wrong?"

Fennel flicked an annoyed glance at me. "Aside from the fact that you're being handed an impossibly profitable internship just because you're rich?"

Swallowing the immediate protests that rose in my throat, I nodded, "Yeah, aside from the privilege."

"I don't get why it's two programs. Why would they give you two programs to access and send your records? That would just be one program."

I looked back at the screen. Maybe they were large files? That didn't really make sense. It would only be a few lines of code for each action.

Inside the sandbox, Fennel opened the program in a code editor. Fennel's eyes jumped down to the start line and began to read the commands. I wasn't as good with code as Fennel. I didn't have to be since I planned to work in modeling and design, but Fennel was going to be a developer. I focused on the developer notes in the code's header.

File Name: RUN1.exe

Developed for proprietary use by MIDAS Tech personnel and interests.

Purpose: This program accesses Breaux Academy records, then pulls and modifies the records for the selected student(s).

That all checked out. I was about to ask Fennel to open the second program in the sandbox to read it, but their expression stopped me. Anger. Disgust. I looked down at the code, trying to decipher the commands. I was slower than Fennel, but I'd get it eventually.

Fennel started to shake their head, almost imperceptibly at first, then harder. "I'm not surprised, but I'm still mad about it."

"What? What is it?" From what I could tell, it did exactly what it said it did. I could see the calls to the student records; I could see the modify statements.

They blew the font size up, startling me from reading the code, and scrolled down to the objects and classes defined after the main body. "Here," they said, pointing to an object. "Those are the student numbers that the code accesses."

The list had six numbers in it and none of them were mine. "So, they sent me the wrong code?"

Fennel shook their head again and scrolled further to another object. They didn't need to tell me what this one was. All Breaux Academy assignments have IDs that start BRAC and Group IDs that start GRP. I had expected the modify statements to add my internship to my school record and update my checklists and planning files for the end of the year, but these were existing assignments in the digital gradebook.

"What does the code do?" I was pretty sure I knew from the look on Fennel's face, from the defeated look in their eyes.

"It swaps the students assigned to these three group projects in the grading database." They're tone was grave.

The icon for the student directory was on my side of the screen, so I opened that and typed in the six student numbers, still visible at the top of the code editor window, separated by semicolons. A short list of records returned as search results. Each record included a student portrait, and Fennel's was right in the middle of the list.

Nothing had come of it, so far. It had been a week since Fennel and I revised the code that Ms. Watkins gave me and ran each program exactly once from my desktop. We'd also restored the files on the card in case I was asked to return it, but the message acknowledging my acceptance had instructed me to dispose of it.

So after Fennel had taken clean copies of the code to add to their personal code library, I wiped and shredded the card into a plastic reuse bin in the print lab. But even after that, I still expected to hear back from MIDAS Tech.

Luckily, our important school work had been completed prior, because I spent more time worrying about it than listening to the lectures. Fennel was pretty sure that if nothing had come of it yet, then nothing ever would, as long as we didn't tell anyone.

They kept reassuring me. "The program we ran threw a common and believable error message, including all of the details aligning with the original code. The only way they could fix it would be to send you a message to ask you to do it again or to change the code, which they don't want to do. They were obviously trying to keep you in the dark about the whole thing."

"Because I wouldn't have gone along with it if I knew." I added.

"Sure, but probably more so that you'd have plausible deniability."

"And now, I have the opposite of that." I leaned further over my knees, my head in my hands. We were sitting in my room, the scene of the not-crime.

Fennel shifted from my desk chair to sit next to me on the bed. They rubbed a hand on my back and gently placed their other on my forearm. "What's the opposite of plausible deniability?"

"Incriminating evidence."

"You don't have any evidence. They literally told you to destroy the evidence."

I looked up miserably through my fingers. "Incriminating knowledge then."

Fennel rolled their eyes. "You don't even know what I did."

My hands fell away from my face. "But I know that you did something. Isn't that enough?"

Fennel opened their mouth to argue, but my desk lit up with an incoming call.

I knew they'd figure it out. My heart hammered in my chest as I waited for the loading ellipsis on the orb to become "MIDAS Tech" or "Watkins, Nilla" or "Audit, Corporate Council" or any of the dozen other names that my worst-case scenarios had provided me. I had to swallow an entire second set of worries when the orb changed to bright blue indicating that the line was a listed contact and the label "Demeter" loaded.

I caught Fennel's gaze. They hopped up from my bed, then immediately ducked down. They dropped to the floor and crawled under my desk, the only place in the room that the sensor didn't pick up. I swapped from my bed to my desk chair, and tried to calm myself by breathing with the orb's pulsing glow. In and out. In and out.

I pulled up to the desk, slightly off center to make sure there was room for Fennel, and tapped the answer button. "Demeter. It's nice to hear from you." My voice cracked, but I could still blame puberty.

Demeter and I looked a lot alike because our mothers looked a lot alike. We also looked a lot like our father's executive assistants for the same reason. Demeter's long, black hair was slicked back into two low, cone-shaped buns. She often wore external data storage devices in her hair, but she usually disguised their shape better. "Hello, Hulk. I don't have much time before my next meeting, but I wanted to call you." Her voice was cool and calm.

Nodding, I tried to smile.

She noticed. She offered a small, kind smile, which made it easier for me to smile back. "I wanted to congratulate you on graduating from the academy and on making the honor list. You didn't receive the highest academic distinction, but I'll admit that you were up against some really outstanding competition." She leaned to the side to show that one of her portrait displays included a screen capture from the awards rally. "I watched the recording on the pod back from Toronto."

That made me happy, even though she didn't watch it live. That might even make me happier, that she went out of her way to find the archived video. She probably had some assistant find it for her, but still. "Yeah, there were some real overachievers in my class." Fennel pinched my calf, and I twitched my leg away from them. I hoped that Demeter didn't notice.

"Yes, like that overachiever friend of yours." She was making fun, though I couldn't tell if the emphasis was on overachiever or friend. "How is Fennel?"

I nodded slowly. "They're good. They're pretty stoked that they made the top distinction, but, I mean, that was pretty much a given with grades like theirs." I fiddled my fingers together on the desk. "They're looking forward to getting out of here and into their internship. I think we all are."

"Fennel's studying to be a developer, right? They've taken all of the coding electives?" Her eyes didn't narrow, but the inner corners of her eyes twitched. It wouldn't have been noticeable except the way the display caught the sheen of the highlighter she applied there.

My stomach sank. This was it. This was the call where it all fell apart. "Yeah." It came out completely monotone.

She hummed, looking away. "I always liked Fennel."

I made a noise in my throat that I hoped the line didn't pick up. Demeter hadn't liked Fennel at all, but she came around after a year or two. I wasn't even sure that dad knew about Fennel or that they were my best friend. I was sure, even when I was thirteen, that he'd tell me to unfriend them, but since it had never come up in conversation, he never got the chance.

Demeter turned her knowing gaze back, pinning me frozen in place. "I expect great things from them." She waited a beat. "And from you." She swallowed, so hard that I could see the collar of her shirt move. When I met her eyes again, she was telling me something important, that she, without a doubt, knew what Fennel and I had done. "The two of you make a good team." She didn't blink. "I'm very proud of you and Fennel and look forward to seeing you both build your careers."

I tried to match her intensity. "Thanks."

She nodded again, once. "Well," the heavy mood lifted so quickly that I questioned if it had even happened, "I have a meeting now, so I have to go."

"Okay."

"Bye."

"Bye."

The line closed and the desk faded back into standby mode. I pushed back away from the desk and looked down at Fennel. They were tucked up into a tight ball under the desk. "I think we did the right thing," they said with a breathy voice.

"Me too," I agreed.

THE URBAN GREENER

Featured Post: Aerogarden Year One Review

Posted by Brant Kade, Retired Master Gardener
Reviewed by Bella Nickel, Alps Small Site Services
Posted 433 days ago, Last Edited 426 days ago.

Well, it's spring again here in GG and it's time to sow the seeds of the next harvest. As I've told you countless times over, a lack of arable soil doesn't mean you can't grow and harvest your own vegetables. We had a lot of success with our aero-garden experiments from last year, and this will be a run-down of those results.

You'll remember the post last year describing how we set up the experimental aero-garden between one of our sustainable living units and our glastic greenhouses. For more information, check out **this link**, and remember to follow our feed for more information on gardening topics. We planted tomatoes, peppers (sweet and hot), and cucumbers and watered them with gray-water run-off from the living unit.

All varieties were from heritage stock grown from cuttings sourced from our usual vendors. I always recommend you throw your hat and your hands in at the local Farming Guild to <u>get your hands on local stock</u>.

Tomatoes: The heritage beefeater and black beauty heritage, a purple flesh variety, performed extremely well in our low gray-water system. The plants stayed healthy and bore big, beautiful fruit. The variety sweet red heritage did not fare as well, and the fruit borne developed cracks and could not be allowed to ripen on the vine.

Peppers: The sweet varietal did fine, though my grandson and I ended up harvesting at least a third of the fruits while still green, allowing the rest to fully ripen into the stunning yellow, orange, and red hues that <u>make a meal pop</u>. The hot peppers struggled with the limited water supplied to their roots and needed supplementation of additional water to make it to maturity. Learning from the experiment, we plan to set up our hot peppers in their own system so additional water can be supplied to those plants without adding that additional water to the entire system.

Cucumbers: Two of the three varieties we planted exceeded our expectations and resulted in fruits both for eating and canning. These canned fruits were enough to last half the winter as a supplement to the usual sturdy root vegetables (potato, carrot, rutabaga) that are a staple of our sustainable winter diets. The final cucumber variety faired well, though the fruits for harvest waned as the season progressed. We have developed an experiment for this season, but you'll have to wait for next week's post to hear about that. (Note, it did not fair badly, but rather seemed to fall short when compared to the abundant harvest of the other two cucumber varieties.)

All told, we are happy with our aero-garden's first year and will add eggplant, pole beans, and musk melon to the limited gray-water system this season.

With love and plants,

Brantpa

Jaywalk

I TAPPED MY PHONE to the tag on the table, waited for the link to load, autofilled my profile, attached my prepared CV, and tapped the sign and submit button at the bottom of the screen.

Jarrod kept shaking his head next to me. "I can't believe you did that, you signed away your future."

I flicked an apologetic glance to the lady sitting behind the table. She wore a big smile, framed by twists that hung from each temple. The rest of her hair was spun up onto itself in a bundle of auburn and red on her head. She looked exactly like the banners and posters around her, complete with the red design accents, bright blue jeans and signature Alps t-shirt. She even wore the same glasses as the associate in the picture.

"Ignore him. He doesn't have the same ambition that I do." I tapped at Jarrod's chest, pushing him away from the table. She nodded a little, obviously used to that sort of thing, which was a shame. As much as the people around here were my family, it felt like they were all looking at the world backwards.

Jarrod huffed and pushed my hand away. "I got plenty of ambition." He looked around the career fair then back at the Alps table. "Don't you think it's creepy though?"

He and I saw the same distinction between the Alps table and the other employers, but we attributed it to different things. He saw the crisp lines of the Alps tablecloth and the bright red banners and signs as an invader among homely tables, while I saw that brilliant branding as a beacon, the most polished presentation in the room. "No, I think that they know what they're doing."

We walked along the row. He stopped to talk to one of the farming guilds. It was clear that they weren't used to the post-secondary students being interested in the work. The man wore ratty overalls and a sun-bleached shirt, at one point it might have been orange but now was pale as dry wheat. "We don't have a website on the corporate network, but I can give you this pamphlet." He handed Jarrod a piece of printed, starched linen folded in half.

It was so old-fashioned, so out-of-date. Why not hire some agency to maintain a website for them? Or pay the fee for a hosting platform to do it? They could at least have some node center cook up a website for the price of a few ads in the margins.

He offered Jarrod a toothy smile, too. "And if you don't need the information, you can use it to patch something."

Taking the pamphlet, Jarrod smiled in return. It was just as big, but far less wrinkled, despite that they weren't that different in age. "Thanks." He opened the pamphlet, scanned down the page, then turned it over. "How would I contact the collective?"

"You'll probably have to drop by one of the meetings. We meet at the outdoor community space at the library every other Tuesday."

I rolled my eyes. Was this guy serious?

The farmer continued. "Most of us don't carry our phones. Those new ones get all messed up in the heat and dust. It just doesn't seem like it's worth the maintenance of them."

"Ah, yeah, I can see that." Jarrod folded the pamphlet up and tucked it into his back pocket. "Thanks for the information. I don't want to promise anyth-"

"No promises needed. My name's Kick." Kick held out his hand; his palm had grown thick, covered in yellowed calluses.

Of course Jarrod took it. "Jarrod."

They nodded the kind of nod that could mean hello or goodbye, then we moved on. I held my phone close to my chest. I hadn't really planned to look at much of the fair, and I still wasn't. I mostly looked at Jarrod.

I watched Jarrod when he charmed the woman at the beekeeping table into two of the free honey samples. I watched Jarrod when he did his little happy dance at ReConstruction's table when he took the little, recycled plastic army man that they offered him. I watched Jarrod when he introduced the young mechanic at the PodWorks table to me as a friend from a few years back, and I watched all the cues that said it had likely been more than just friends.

And to myself, I wished that maybe it would make it easier to break up with him.

"Hey, Jaywalk, I think we're boring your friend." The mechanic turned his almost-red-brown eyes at me, smiling a little smaller than before.

Jarrod apologized to me, to the mechanic, then we moved on again.

Looking back, I'd realize that he didn't correct him like he usually did when people called me his friend. He didn't kindly say, "Girlfriend, actually", before moving on.

If it had been just me, I would have been in and out of the fair in 10 minutes. Since I'd been with Jarrod it took almost two hours, so we headed right over to Stella's Diner, only a few blocks away from the equity center campus. Jarrod liked to tease me that we were going to *my* diner, but I was named Stella after the children's book, not as a legacy.

We ordered our usual, a milkshake and the Number 6, which came with a cheeseburger, fries, and a milkshake already. We ordered one cherry and one malt vanilla. Leigh knew to bring it out separately, so that I had the cherry shake and fries, and Jarrod got the cheeseburger and malt vanilla.

I didn't know what to say, so I ate instead.

Before Jarrod, I'd had boyfriends, but none of them had been like Jarrod. Breaking up with them had been made so easy by their attitudes, faults, mistakes.

One of my boyfriends had cheated on me and then made up an elaborate lie to cover it up, maxing out one of his credit cards, buying pod tickets half-way across the world, and pretending to be visiting his mother in British Columbia. His mother was the one that told me. She saw his post about it, and called him out. Another had been so rude to my older sister that I couldn't stand to look at him. He'd disrespected her home, turned his nose up at her food and hospitality, and even talked down to her about her research at the Corporate Science Institute.

In contrast, Jarrod was perfect. I wanted to pack him up and take him with me to the suburbs, keep him forever, but that just wasn't how it was going to be. I wanted something so different than he wanted, and I couldn't ask him to give that up.

Frustrated, I sucked the thick shake through the pulp straw harder than before, earning a twinge of pain in my temples.

Jarrod pushed his plate, now that all that was left of the burger were crumbs, away from him and turned his focus to his half melted shake. He centered the old-style milkshake glass in front of him and stirred the vanilla around. "So, I want to go on one more date."

I blinked at him. "What did you just say?"

He huffed, suddenly sheepish. "I said that I want you to promise to go on one more date with me." Satisfied with himself, he dipped down to take a easy, half melted sip of his shake.

Anger and betrayal bubbled up my throat. "What are you trying to say?" As soon as I shouted, I regretted it.

There weren't other patrons in the place, but the workers were there, and they would tell someone who would tell someone until everyone would know that Jarrod and I weren't a thing anymore. And I regretted it because I had just been thinking about breaking up with him. Why was I so angry that he had found the words before I did? Embarrassment settled into my gut. Because he'd beat me to it, because he was dumping me instead of the other way around.

Worst of all, he didn't look surprised at the outburst. He just drank his shake some more, his eyes looking out the window at the blue-green sky. "My mom thinks I'm stupid for it." He spoke to the window, calm as always. "She really likes you," he tilted his head, looking at me sweetly.

If he wasn't embarrassed, then I didn't need to be either; I pushed it down. "I like your mom. She's always making sure to send leftover food with me."

"Yeah." He nodded. "And, I don't think us breaking up has to change the way you and her are."

I wasn't sure about that, but I wanted it to be true. "Your mom doesn't like the centers either, though." I crossed my arms on the table, pushing the shake away from me.

He pressed his lips together. "You're right."

Neither of us responded for a bit. He watched the sky; I watched him. I dragged in a breath, then pushed it back out. I untucked my arms, collected our plates and took them to the counter, where Leigh was pretending to be self-conscious about listening in on our conversation. It would have been more convincing if they weren't looking at me with so much concern. I pinched my lips at them, daring them to pity me.

I kept my eyes trained on them as I turned back around, but I was startled by Jarrod standing behind me. Caught awkwardly between him and the counter, I waited while he paid for our meal.

He wasn't afraid of me or himself or the world. From my vantage, I looked over his jaw line. His jaw was squarer than when we'd first gotten together almost 3 years ago, but I still expected it to get squarer, for him to grow more handsome. He had a few pimples on his face, where his smile lines were already starting to form.

I'd never been dumped before. Was this what being dumped was like?

Leigh handed his phone back, and he slipped it into his pants pocket. He waved, smiled at them, and scooted around me and the stools to make his way down the diner's narrow aisle.

I was being left behind. I felt a stab of guilt for the boys I'd dumped. I felt a pang of sympathy for the other people Jarrod had dumped. We were all in the same club now, a club that I can't imagine any of us wanted to be in.

"Hey?" Leigh's hand touched my arm. They leaned on the counter, nodding a little at me. "You'll be alright."

Where I expected disdain, a sinking feeling settled in. This was going to be the end of the best thing in my life. Then suddenly I was frustrated, so frustrated, at myself. This was ending so that I could go to the suburbs, to work at Alps, to feel like I was part of something. I nodded to Leigh, hoping I convinced them that I'd be okay.

There was a knock on the window. Jarrod's muffled voice called, "Hey!" He tapped his knuckle to the window again. "This date isn't over yet." He looked at me expectantly, eyes shining.

He walked me to his grandparents' house, and we borrowed his grandad's truck. It was a construction truck, so it was more dirt than metal. He offered me a towel to sit on in the front seat and drove us out of town.

Had it been anyone else, any of my other boyfriends, any of my previous crushes, I would have worried that he was driving me out to the middle of nowhere to murder me. I would probably have still gone with any one of those other people, but I would've been worried for my life. With

Jarrod, the thought barely occurs to me, even though we just broke up. There just isn't anything in him not to trust.

Keeping his eyes on the road, Jarrod bobbed his head toward me. "I want to show you something nice. I think you're going to think it's not nice, but I need you to know that I think it's nice."

He had plump lips that I might never get to kiss again, probably never kiss again. They moved around his words, and I couldn't help but watch them. "Are you going to tell me more?"

Humming a little, he raised his eyebrows in an amused, mum expression.

I turned my gaze out the window, seeing the yellow fields blur. I propped my elbow against the base of the truck's window and leaned my cheek on my hand. "Of course not. You love having secrets."

"Surprises," he corrects. "I don't keep secrets."

We rode for a while in silence. The further out of town we rode, the more things seemed to yellow under the unfiltered light, but it made the sky seem bluer in comparison.

He turned off the road onto a gravel drive. "This is where my aunt and uncle live, on my mom's side."

I'd met his mom's sister once at a family event in August last year. One of the Kade cousins had a birthday, and

Jarrod brought me along as his plus one. I'd been out of my depth for most of it, but I had a great time. Since August, Jarrod's aunt had swapped houses with his granddad. Jarrod had offered to help, but his mom had insisted on prioritizing our winter semester examinations. I was grateful for the excuse, but Jarrod hadn't liked being told to sit it out.

His granddad had some health problems, so living closer to the doctor's office and podlines was worthwhile, though he still made his way out to the family fields to check on the crops and gardens. I'd been to visit his grandad a few times with him in the spring semester. They had the same smile, and the same sense of humor. I wondered if one day Jarrod would have the same wrinkles around his eyes.

The gravel driveway was the most defined path on the property, but there were various dirt paths that split off, made by large tractor tires into the fields. There were some places where a path hadn't formed yet, but the grass at the edge of the driveway's manicured strip was bent in a reminiscent pattern. Up near the old barn but still a ways from the house, Jarrod turned off the driveway to follow a mown strip of land where a line of wire towers stood, reaching out into the distance.

I looked over my shoulder. I glanced at the house, wondering if his aunt and uncle knew we were coming, then continued my sweep to follow the lines backward to the hazy spot on the horizon.

"And, we're here." Jarrod rolled the old truck to a gentle stop. "Well, we're where I'm going to park." He turned a grin to me, turning the key to stop the ignition, but left the keys to dangle there. "Come on."

I grimaced down at my shoes and outfit. I had not dressed for tromping around a farmer's field; I was wearing a puffy-sleeved top, dark purple slacks, and a pair of sensible, purple heels. I was specifically dressed for a career fair.

Jarrod opened my door. He was not usually this gentleman-ly. Part of me thought he was hurrying me; another thought maybe he was on his best behavior for our last date, that he was treating me so politely because we were broken up now. When I didn't jump out, his eyebrows furrowed with confusion, then concern, then mild realization.

I raised an eyebrow, when his eyes lit back up.

He pulled open the half-size door to the truck's cramped second row seating and rooted around for a bit. "I think I've got some old boots back here."

Pursing my lips, I shook my head up to the sky in a kind of defeat.

"Got one." He blindly handed me a dirty, black rubber boot around the truck cab's frame.

I caught it before it got dirt on my nice shirt or the towel I was sitting on. In the same calm defeat, I removed my heels and tucked them up at the console to avoid scuffing them. I slid my left foot into the boot and carefully tucked my pants leg into it. He was ready with the other when I'd finished.

His grin was contagious, so even though I felt awkward in the too-big-boots in the squishy field, I felt the ends of my mouth tug outward.

Beyond some gravel and rock piles that looked to be extra from when the transmission towers were first installed, we made our way up a slope to the top of a little hill at the edge of the field. If we followed the same path further, we'd start climbing the more intense incline of the mountain on the back half of the property. In front of us, most of the mountain was covered in forest and a neverending layer of fallen leaves from years of autumns piling onto each other, except for the manicured strip cut through for the towers.

Jarrod sucked in a big breath through his nose. "I love how it smells up here." He closed his eyes and breathed the same way again.

My eyes followed the lines from tower to tower up the mountain until they disappeared over it to the other side. They were so old-fashioned. Most tech was wireless, but the lines were obviously maintained. They stood like giant trees, acting as a bridge between the digital and natural landscapes.

"Yeah, they ruined the view when they put these things in, but I just don't look that way anymore, you know?"

I turned back to him. He had fixed a hard look at the towers. His eyes looked exhausted. "But that's not what I brought you up here for." The tension in his face went slack, relaxed and open as he spun us both back to the direction we'd come up from.

―●―

To the side, under a tree that stood at the edge of the forested mountain, there was a stone bench. He led the way over to it, sat down, and gestured broadly for me to join him. "You're being quiet."

"I.." I patted my thighs, "I don't know what to say."

He nodded. "That makes sense."

"We just broke up?" I sounded like a child who had to put away their tablet for bedtime. The tone was reminiscent of the usual pleas for just five more minutes.

"Yeah," he didn't look at me, just looked out at the property.

Taking his lead, I looked out too, but there wasn't much to look at. There was a field, a barn, a treeline separating the next field from this one. My eyes were drawn back to the transmission towers instead. We sat in silence for a few long seconds.

"So, I wanted to show you this." He sounded far away.

"I figured."

"This is where my grandmother is buried."

Just when I'd started to find words again, he blew them all away.

"She'd told mom that she didn't want something so useless as a headstone, so after we buried her, mom bought this stone bench." He smoothed one of his hands over the stone. "I think it's kinda brilliant, like why don't other people have benches on their graves. It's more inviting this way."

As I settled with the words, I found that I liked the idea, too. The silence stretched between us. "So, did you want to introduce your ex-girlfriend to your grandmother?" I asked as softly as I could.

He shook his head and sat up straighter. "No, I wanted to show you because I want to be buried here." He finally looked at me again.

"What?" My voice came out louder than I'd expected it to.

He was determined, I could see it in the slight ridge between his eyebrows. "I want to be buried here, and I wanted to ask you if you wanted to be buried here, too."

I felt struck under his gaze. I could feel where his warm, brown eyes bore into my skin. My chest grew hot with a swirling emotion between concern and appall. I leaned away, peering at him from behind a raised shoulder. "Are you dying?" My eyes flicked down to his knees, then assessed him on their way back up to his face.

He looked fine other than his indignant look. "What? No!" He waved my question away.

"Are you sick?" I rocked a little further away from him.

"No," he insisted. He reached out a hand and covered mine, where they were clasped tightly in my lap.

My body relaxed automatically, paying no attention to the topic, paying no mind to the fact that he'd broken up with me. I liked his hands. They were bigger than mine, fuller. His fingers were thick and strong in the way that my typist hands weren't.

He scanned the property spread out before us, rubbing his other hand over his mouth in thought. It fell away. "I love you."

My hands flew out from under his, gripping the air like it held something that I desperately needed. "What is wrong with you?!" I was shouting now. I stood up, and his hand fell from my thigh. "First you tell me that we're ending this," I ticked off a finger at him, "then you ask me to be buried beside you," another finger, "then you tell me that you love me?!"

"It's not the first time I told you I loved you." It looked like he genuinely thought that would be a helpful thing to say.

I glowered at him and shouted again, "What is going on?!"

"I was trying to explain." The high emotions that I was putting out were starting to affect him. His usual, easy-going demeanor was growing thicker, his movements more enunciated.

"You weren't explaining anything! You hit me with it. One, two, three. Like it was something obvious." I stamped a foot, but it was lost in the oversized boot.

His eyebrows were furrowed. His eyes were closed. His jaw was clenched. "I was getting to it."

I huffed out an aggravated breath. "Do it again," I demanded. "In a better order." I dropped back down next to him and crossed my arms defensively. "In lots of small words, so I understand what's going on." I didn't look at him yet. I blew out another angry puff of air, trying to regulate myself.

This man was so aggravating.

I turned to look at him again.

But, I was completely in love with him.

The setting reminded me all at once why I followed him out here on a whim in the wrong clothes. The sun caught the curls falling just over his eyes. He was pursing his lips in frustration, and his face was scrunched together in thought. I could almost see the neurons firing, the nodes cobbling together something for me, just for me, just from him.

A bead of sweat ran down his face from his hairline to his chin.

He sucked in a big breath, then sagged under the weight of its release. "I love you, Stella." He turned big, emotional eyes at me. It wasn't a ploy or anything. He was just like that, genuine about everything. "But, I won't be happy with you at the center." He sighed lightly, "And, you can't stand the idea of living out here." He lifted his shoulders up and sheepishly looked back out to the field. "Not because I don't love you, and not because you don't love me. Just because we're not meant for that."

When my bottom lip wobbled, I bit into it hard to stabilize it. I wanted to argue that if we loved each other, that if he loved me, that it shouldn't matter if we lived at the center, but I knew that if that were true, then I should've been willing to live out here with him. And, I wasn't. I was sure that I was supposed to go to the center, that I'd find my purpose, my future, there. And, he was perfectly content out here.

"But," there was a lilt to his voice, like he thought he was funny, "Just because you couldn't stand to live out here, doesn't mean you wouldn't be caught dead out here."

Even after a sentence like that, I didn't worry that he was going to kill me. That's how head-over-boots I was for Jarrod Kade. I leveled a look at him, reminding him that I still needed him to use lots of little words to explain whatever strange idea he was trying to get at.

He held out a cajoling hand, "Now, I know what you're thinking. Your future is at the center, but do you even know what they do with dead people at the center?"

I narrowed my eyes at him further, but my crossed arms slumped because, no, I hadn't thought to look it up. I shook my head, barely.

"They just burn them at the center, like in the center's power facility, for power." His fingers fidgeted. "Where's the reverence in that? How would someone visit you?"

"How would someone remember you?" I echoed. "I imagine there would be a stone somewhere." But even as

I said it, I realized that the suburbs didn't have cemeteries. I'd taken full tours of Typhon Ridge and Samara Village, and neither had included anything that resembled death facilities.

"So, maybe your stone goes here." He tried again; he was being soft with me. His face was completely slack, waiting for an answer, looking like he was prepared to wait a long time.

But I couldn't leave that lovely face waiting. I was reminded of the first time he told me he loved me. When he had taken my hand gently, after we'd been dancing so hard we were out of breath, he leaned into my ear to tell me, and even without my breath, I'd blurted it back to him. It felt so long ago, so separate from where we were.

"Maybe my stone goes here." I agreed.

He grinned wide.

I rolled my eyes at him. "But what does that mean? What do you think having my stone out here means?"

"That you'll have to come back," he said matter-of-fact. "You'll have to show your face around here every once in a while." He relaxed into his breath.

He was right, but I wasn't going to tell him that. I might love him, but no one actually admits to someone that they're right. I watched him watch the treeline. "Why didn't you just ask me to come back to visit? Why did you have to bring your grandmother into this?" I patted the bench.

He laughed. "Because you would have said no." He shook his head, tilted his chin down, and shot me a 'tell me I'm wrong' look. "You have a very strict plan. The plan is to finish your degree, find a job placement at a center, and move to the suburbs. There was no room for you to come back, no reason to. You've got all the steps figured out. I knew I'd have to work my way back from the end instead." He looked smug now.

"Back from the end?" Oh no.

"Yeah, like now I can try to talk you into retiring out here. I mean, how else would we be ready for you to be buried here?"

I was incredulous, and I didn't hide my emotions very well, so he had to be aware of it.

He continued, grinning cheekily. "And, if you're retiring out here, why not do some part time for a bit at the end of your processing career? You could do two processing days and teach at the equity center."

Shaking my head, I stood up to walk away from him.

He was so aggravating.

"Then," he followed me down toward the truck, "You probably need to prep for that by taking some classes. And, I know that there are fancy classes on the net or in the suburbs, but they aren't like out here. It's different tech and a different culture. Let alone, you could get some admission fees waived since you already attended." Now, he sounded mostly like he was joking. So full of himself.

I stomped the boots, making squelching noises in the muddy field. I hoped his boots would be extra mucked up after this.

Jarrod caught up to me, edged out in front of me, then blocked me, giddy with happiness. With the sun hitting him at a perfect angle, he was gorgeous.

And I was furious. "I'm breaking up with you." In that moment, I wanted it to hurt him, but it stung me instead. I bit at the inside of my cheek, unsure what to say next.

He took each of my forearms, grounding me and holding me at a precious distance. "I know." He was still smiling a kind of sad smile that was still hopeful at the edges and under the eyes. "And we have to break up. We have to move on, do our own things," he nodded to me and to himself, "then, when the time comes, we'll be buried out here together. Yeah?"

I could see it. I could see all the different ways that it could happen; all the different lives that I could live. I saw one where, as per the instructions in my will, an urn and stone were shipped back to the farmhouse, and one where I only did half time at the processing center so I could raise kids out here, and one where I fell in love in the suburbs but brought him back with me and settled all of us here together. There were so many paths back, where there had only ever been one path out. It was so sad, and so much, and I felt more lost than I had ever felt before.

"Yeah," I agreed, "we'll be buried here together."

IN NEWS AND UPCOMING EVENTS

NationAlive joins Alps in Multimillion Dollar Partnership

Covered by Kellem Hall, Alps Journalism and Interviews
Reviewed by Jaxon Treau, Alps News and Blogs
Posted 177 days ago, Last Edited 172 days ago

Alps and NationAlive are bringing big changes to healthcare, domestically and abroad. The two companies have held contracts for many years. NationAlive runs portions of its software on Alps' processing centers, and Alps offers a host of NationAlive's medical, dental, optical, and pet services as benefits to their employees. Now, the two companies have entered a mutual partnership.

But what does this partnership mean for you?

The Corporate Council has three different terms for these kinds of dealings. Acquisition is used to describe when one company is purchased or absorbed by another.

Acquisitions result in the absorber's CEO, COO, and Board of Directors assuming management and control of the acquisition's employees and assets. Merger describes two company's pooling resources and assets under one name, but some management and control from each entity remains in the new structure. Partnership describes when two companies enter mutually exclusive contracts with each other, but otherwise maintain their separate management and control entities.

> Alps and NationAlive have entered this partnership at the beginning of the Fiscal Summer, the period of time when associates across corporate entities take time away from the workplace to connect with nature or loved ones. Steven Benedict promises big changes when the associates return. "I'm excited to devote our resources to such a worthwhile cause. Healthcare and mental health are often overlooked, and I want to make sure that our associates greet every day with a smile."

Will Devros has yet to make a public announcement on the partnership, but in a press conference for

HRDev, Demeter Devros entertained a question on the topic, "NationAlive, like HRDev, has made it their mission to put people first. We take care of frontline workers across industries. This partnership follows our shared, ever-present strategy to make our solutions more human."

Both companies will maintain their chairs on the Corporate Council.

Tether

I wasn't paid enough. I wasn't paid enough to buy the lunches offered in the downstairs cafeteria. I wasn't paid enough to stay late to process data files when they were turned in after the close-of-business deadline. I wasn't paid enough to use the health insurance that the Corporate Council's Research Division offered.

So, surely, I wasn't paid enough to care that the research assistant at the station across from me was crying.

At first, I just figured that she had a bit of a runny nose from the chill of the lab. She was sniffing a lot, but when I peeked around my upright screen, I caught the slightest glimpse of her tear-stained cheeks.

And now it was just plain distracting.

I didn't want to catch her eye, so I trained my gaze on my own desktop screen. But as the sniffing continued, I started to wonder if I was supposed to ask her about it.

People only cried in public when they wanted to talk about it, right? Then again, was an otherwise empty research lab during off-hours public?

"Uh, are you okay?"

Sniff. "I'm optimal."

I wasn't paid enough to care, and yet I did. "But...you're crying."

She laughed. "Yeah, but it's fine. It's just that," sniff, "I can't even remember what I'm crying about."

I wasn't sure what that could mean. I tapped at my workstation, opening the personnel directory. "You don't remember what you're crying about?" I looked up my own desk number, B-2-07, and opened the directory entry, Terrence Walker. Alongside sections for contact info, team registrations, education, and awards, there was a tab that listed other personnel that I worked with. On that tab, there was a list of the usual suspects, Thomas, Platty, Geiger, all personnel assigned to the sleep study project, all marked with a gray indicator that they weren't logged in.

When I looked up again, she was staring at me. I flicked my eyes away from her teary gaze, busying myself with my workstation. I shifted the window to the far edge of my screen and selected the data window to ensure that it still showed that I was actively working.

Peeking back to her, I realized she wasn't looking at me. She was looking through me. "Are you sure you're okay?" I started to stand up. "I can take you to the health unit downstairs."

"Hmm?" Her eyes came back into focus. "Oh, no, I'm fine, really." She waved it off and turned back to her own screen.

The personnel system hadn't picked up on our conversation yet. I racked my brain for a topic, something to ask her. "You could use the online health check in if you'd rather." I cringed inwardly. I would hate to be given that advice.

As did she. "No thank you," she said it louder than anything before.

When I met her eyes that time, her hard look told me that she thought the new NationAlive software was just as bullshit as I did. But neither of us said it, because it wasn't something you said.

"I get that." I tried to match her volume, though it felt weird to talk that loudly in a room full of empty workstations. "So, what brings you in on a Sunday?"

Her gaze hardened further. "I'm not interested."

"What? In a conversation?"

"In whatever this is."

"I'm just worried that you're crying at your workstation."

"And...I told you that it was nothing." She scooted her rolling stool over to the other end of her workstation, so she was blocked by the upright screens.

The directory application refreshed. A new name appeared at the top. Thalia Hess (she/her). "You expect me to see someone crying and ignore it?" I opened her directory entry. Part of me expected that her personal information page would be empty. Mine was. I had been onboarded just before they started making everyone fill it out in the orientation session. Her entry was still sparse, but it listed her start date, location, degrees and certifications, vertical managers, and project name. She was assigned to the mental health project.

She was quiet.

I clicked on the project name for more information. *The Corporate Mental Health Project (CMHP) seeks to understand the effects of various states of mental health on processing capability.* It seemed that whoever made the entry had been just as invested as I would have been.

We weren't paid enough to care about this.

A red band flashed on at the border of my screen along with a scrolling banner along the top, 'Associate has been clocked out due to prolonged unchargeable activity'. I huffed, switching my active window back to the data window at the center of the workstation. The alert lingered until I scrolled in the file and made a note in the note field.

Considering she'd checked out of our conversation, I tried to, as well. I read each line of data and made my notes in the file. Using processors to process data always came with risk, an inherent bias, which made it nearly useless in the research field. The human touch that processing brought to projects was key in many fields like design and copywriting and legal matters, but it wasn't necessary or even accepted in the research-

She sniffed, still crying.

I tapped the down button to my next annotation cell. I typed my annotation.

She sniffed again.

"So, what's your name?" I glanced back to the directory window, but didn't move my cursor, just kept typing in my annotation.

She let out a sob.

I jumped up from my stool and looked over the monitors to her. She was bent over the workspace, her face in her hands. I could see the slight glow of the red border on her screen bouncing off her slick, white workspace. "What's wrong?" I wasn't sure what to do.

My partner, Michel, was much better at all of this than I was. He was the kind of person that could sidle up to you, ask really personal questions without it seeming like he was prying, and rub your back until you felt better. If one of our friends came over to talk through something, I wasn't even allowed in the same room. Most times, he'd go so far as to send me off on errands, collect some groceries from the commissary, sign us up for a volunteer shift at the neighborhood CO_2 collection site, take something we'd checked out of the item library back to the local branch, that kind of thing. Anything to get me out of the house.

I stepped away from my workspace, the red border appearing on my screen again. The workspaces occupied a continuous counter, so I had to walk all the way to the end of the row then back to her. And even though I had a good fifteen seconds to figure out what I was going to do, I still hadn't come up with anything by the time I was standing next to her.

When she looked up at me, her makeup was running; there was snot leaking from her nose and tracks of eyeliner down her face. "I think," hic, "I'm just stressed?"

She was asking me, and I had no clue what to do or say. I wasn't cut out for this. "You think?"

That was the wrong thing to say. She burst into a new round of tears. I was really shit at this. I dug my phone from my pocket and swiped at the screen to unlock it. I had to accept the terms pop-up to use the facility's network before the phone would open, and when it did, most of my apps were grayed out, unavailable to me under the agreement.

I opened the favorites bar and long-tapped on Michel's contact icon to call him.

"What are you doing?" Thalia managed between breaths.

I kinda shrugged, but mostly I was frozen there, staring past my phone at the leg of her workspace.

Michel answered after the third trill. "Hey, I thought you were still at work?" His eyebrows shot up when he took in my appearance.

"Hi." My eyes refocused on the screen. I was completely red in the face, feeling inadequate and unprepared for the situation. "This is Thalia. She works here."

"What?" Michel, understandably confused.

"Huh?" Thalia, still crying.

I turned the phone around so they could see each other.

Thalia stared at the phone screen. She didn't look upset. Actually, she looked very upset; she looked like she was crying her eyes out in the middle of the research facility, but the phone thrust into her face didn't make it worse.

"Ah," Michel understood. There was a shifting sound on the other end, he was probably making himself comfortable on our couch. "Are you okay?"

Thalia rolled her eyes. "Yeah, I'm fine." She picked herself up from her workspace and rubbed her hands over her face to wipe away any active tears.

"You don't look fine." Michel used to be a therapist in what he referred to as his previous life. He'd worked for a small telehealth network contracted with some big-name healthcare companies. He'd loved his work and meeting with patients. We both liked to dig into something to find out how it worked, but he had a softer touch, working with people, than I did, berating millions of records of data. It was something he was truly good at. "Can you tell me what you're feeling?"

"Did you call the telehealth check-in?" She scrutinized the screen through her tears. "It's crazy how realistic these AIs are."

I shook my head. Of course not, the AI for our health system didn't have a face yet. "No, it's my husband." This was awkward. I flicked my eyes away from Thalia. I looked at the frosted windows, glowing from the sunshine beyond.

"Oh." She turned back to the phone, still trying to correct her appearance. "Sorry, hi." She sniffed. "I'm fine really. I don't need-"

"You do." Michel said it in that way that only your mother or your family's beloved doctor could.

She was taken aback, then she nodded to herself. "I do," she agreed.

Was I supposed to stand here holding the phone out? I glared at the window, then flicked my eyes to the ceiling, then to the floor.

"So...what's going on?" I couldn't see Michel, but I could picture his look of concern.

"I don't know." She gritted the words out. "I don't remember why I'm sad."

My arm was starting to feel tired.

"You don't remember?"

She was quiet for a bit before responding, "No."

Then my arm was really starting to ache. I pushed the phone toward Thalia, and she rushed to grab it before I shoved it into her. She sniffed again, and propped the phone up on her workspace, spinning her stool to speak to it. "Well, I know why I'm crying, but not *why* I'm crying," she sighed, "I don't even know how to say this without breaching any of the research policies." She squeezed her eyes tight in frustration; new tears dripped down from her lashes.

"Hold on, I can log in and swap onto a corporate line."

Sniff. "You work here too?"

"Yep." There was the familiar plucking sound of screen tapping on the other end of the line.

I shoved my hands into my pockets. Now what was I supposed to do? Go for a walk? Go back to my workspace?

An echoing ding signified the call being swapped onto a corporate line. "Everything said on this line is recorded and confidential, ultimately property of the Corporate Council's Research Division." He cleared his throat. "We're required to say that."

After Michel lost his telehealth job, he applied to everything outside of the Corporate Research Division that came his way. We had the Typhon Ridge membership fee that we were still on the hook for, after all. And he was selected for some of the positions, lots of week-long trial periods leaving him exhausted. If it had been any other role but user research, he probably wouldn't have applied for it. But he did, so now we commuted together at least two days a week, like so many other families from our suburb.

I shuffled my feet, wondering if I should sit on the stool for the workspace next to her. That also didn't seem like the right thing to do.

"So, tell me what's going on?" His voice sounded like his eyebrows were scrunched down in the middle. He sounded like he'd crossed one leg over the other at the knee and placed his clasped fingers on top.

Thalia sniffed again, but she drew it in longer than the other ones. "I work on the mental health project."

This was so awkward, and not something I needed to know. I scuffed my shoes as I walked away down the line of workspaces. I considered pacing the far wall or walking laps around the room.

It wasn't like my work was a high priority; it could wait until tomorrow. I could just pack up and leave but Thalia had my phone. I wasn't paid enough for this.

"Our findings indicate that better mental health leads to better processing, so we've been working with coders to set up mental health checks during processing time."

"What?!" The calm image of Michel I'd had in my head vanished, replaced by a worried Michel with his hands retracted into fists just above where they'd sat on his legs. "Did you..."

Sniff. "Yeah, I tried it on myself."

Traveling back to the house felt like forever. Thalia and I sat diagonally from each other on a commuter bus to Typhon's Ridge. The buses were self-driving, using markings on the road to guide them. They were basically the same as the pods, except for their size.

Thalia didn't live in Typhon's Ridge. According to her bus pass, she lived in one of the older condo developments closer to the center, so I used one of our visitor swipes to get her onto the bus. It would also enable her to go home afterward via the bus or a community pod.

She was still crying, hiccuping at the window where she watched the scenery pass by. Aside from the crying, she was pretty, with a prominent nose and strong cheekbones. In fact, the red on her nose and around her eyes seemed to compliment her look, adding color to her otherwise pale skin. There was still some evidence of the tracks of eyeliner on her cheeks.

Should I say something? The only other people on the bus were some older, primary students in the front rows, giggling about the recreation class they'd gone to.

I tilted my head back to stare at the bus' roof.

"So, how did you two meet?"

It was so soft, that I doubted that she'd actually asked. I stared for a moment, before catching her eyes in her reflection, a watery, expectant look. "He was my therapist," I shrugged and slumped into the seat.

"Therapist?" It was far away, like she was outside with the manicured patches of grass and running trails. "I can't imagine how that went. He was your therapist?"

"Yeah. It's a long story." One I didn't want to share with her. It had been a shit show. I was seeing a therapist, then I started having feelings for the therapist, then I requested a transfer to a different therapist, then after like six other therapists, I was fed up with the fact that none of the other therapists were compatible with me, then I was randomly assigned back to Michel. And then he'd asked me why I'd requested a transfer in the smallest, most vulnerable voice I'd ever heard. My ears burned just thinking about it. "Too long actually."

She nodded, sniffing again.

The bus pulled up to the stop at the end of my street. Like most of the other streets, it was a short branch from the main road ending in a small cul-de-sac for the pods to loop around. I signaled to Thalia that it was our stop, so we both stood.

The recording over the speakers reminded us to collect all our belongings before we debarked, but neither of us had any additional belongings, just phones in our pockets. I swiped my phone over the pad at the front.

"Mr. Walker?" One of the kids leaned forward in his seat, grabbing the rail in front of him. "Did you work again today?" I recognized him vaguely, but I didn't know who he was. Michel would know; he'd know in an instant who the kid was, which street he lived on, where his parents worked, all of it.

"Yeah, I did." I nodded politely, hoping that was all I had to do.

The kid shook his head at me and pursed his lips. "You work too much, Mr. Walker. My mom says you go in to avoid her."

Okay. I knew exactly who it was. It was our neighbor's kid.

"Maybe I do." I really didn't like that neighbor; she was always asking us to go with her on errands and such, then if we did, she used the time to complain about her husband to Michel's sympathetic ear.

The kid grinned. "I knew you didn't like her." Around him, his friends cooed, clapping him on the back and looking back and forth between us.

I rolled my eyes, then climbed down the steps.

"Hey, Mr. Walker, I get it though." He'd leaned over the bar, blocking Thalia from following me. He turned his head and looked over Thalia once, taking in her teary face. "You look awful," he made a face at me as he sank back into his seat.

I offered my tight, neighborly smile and nodded back to dismiss him. I led the way down the street.

"Who was that?"

I squinted my eyes at Thalia. Earlier, she hadn't wanted anything to do with me, but now she was all chatty. Admittedly, that was usually what happened when people realized that I was married to Michel.

We walked the rest of the way in silence. Our house looked like all the other houses, so much so that I always checked the number on the front before walking up to the door. I swiped my phone over the lock pad and pushed the door open. "Hey, Michel, we're here!"

Thalia crowded in behind me.

There was no coat to take from her, nothing to hang on the hooks lining the entryway. I smoothed my hands over my khaki-colored denims. "Uh, do you want a drink or something?"

She nodded slightly to me, but her eyes caught on Michel, who had brought her a glass of water without asking first. I shoved my hands into my pockets.

"Hi Thalia, it's nice to meet you in person," Michel offered a warm smile. He and Thalia were about the same height, so when he gently touched her forearm, it didn't look as awkward as it would've if I'd done it. "Let's get set up in my home office."

Thalia followed him, and I followed Thalia.

Michel showed Thalia the office, a room that was marketed as a guest room on the community's site page. We'd only ever had one guest, Michel's youngest sister, and she'd stayed on our couch for four painful and worrisome days. Michel had split ties with his family when he'd transitioned, so her staying here had been a wreck. Michel had some friends from secondary school, but they didn't come here to the house. We didn't have enough visitor passes for that kind of thing.

"Please, take a seat wherever you like." Michel motioned to the couch and chairs.

I stood in the door, waiting for my cue to leave, my errand to run.

Thalia swallowed and sat in one of the chairs. It was a faux leather chair that you sunk into when you sat on it. "So, you said you needed to see me in person to fix this?"

Michel nodded. "Even though I'm not currently practicing, I'm still a licensed therapist. I pay my recert each year." He pointed up to the electronic frame with his license displayed. "So, can you tell me what happened?"

Was I supposed to stand here?

"I told you. We wanted to add mental health checks to the processing programming, and when I tested it, something went wrong." Thalia breathed deeply, deliberately. She wasn't crying, but she seemed to be holding it back.

Michel scooted forward to the edge of his chair. "How does the check module work?"

Thalia's nose twitched. "I don't know. I'm not the programmer."

"What is it supposed to do?"

"If a processor seems stressed, it checks on it. It checks for the usual signs of stress, spikes of adrenaline, cortisol, blood pressure, heart rate, then it checks in on the processor."

It all seemed straight forward to me.

Michel pinched the bridge of his nose, so it must not have been as straight forward as it seemed. He sucked in an agitated breath, then pushed it out, then looked at me, mouthing the words, "I really hate processing."

He stood up and opened a cabinet behind his desk. He lifted the helmet from the charging rack and carried it carefully over to Thalia. "This is an older model, but it is certified and runs the latest version of the Think-Tree software. It doesn't run any other software." He pulled up the specs on his desk screen for Thalia to look at, but she wasn't interested, staring instead into her hands in her lap.

Michel looked like he politely wanted to throttle something. Not Thalia. I knew what Michel hated about processing more than anyone else in the world, and I didn't disagree with any of it, but it was such a hard thing to wrap my head around. It wasn't like I was a therapist or anything, but I worked with data, so I understood that part at least.

Thalia looked up, tears were welled up in her eyes, but they hadn't leaked down her face yet. "Do you deal with this a lot?"

He sucked at the seam of his lips.

"He's like a doula." I offered, not knowing if I was helping or not. They were both looking at me with big, doey eyes. It looked like I was a part of whatever this was. "He helps people transition from processing back into normal life."

"On the side," he added. "I work as a user researcher for the Corporate Research Division, but my hours are funky, so I still do this," he handed her the helmet, "on the side." He stepped away back to his desktop. "Processing can do some nasty stuff to a person, so I try to undo what I can." He offered a grin to her over his shoulder, before focusing his attention at the screen.

I came forward, standing next to him, towering over both of them, scrutinizing Think-Tree's start-up screen.

"You're too tall," he grumbled at me, then yanked at my belt loop, "sit down."

So I did.

Michel typed in his passwords and authenticated the software connection. "So, had you processed before?" He waved a hand at her. "You can put the helmet on."

Thalia did. "Yeah, I did some part-time work while I finished up my white-collar certifications."

White collar? I hadn't seen any white-collar certs on her directory page, maybe it wasn't as filled out as I thought it had been.

"Oh, what did you cert in?" Michel opened a new environment in the Think-Tree file, saved it into the Think-Tree system with the standard naming convention, then connected the helmet that was still offline to the environment.

The software looked a lot like a programming application, and that was probably because in many ways it was. I worked in M Code and AEX, and no matter what software I used to script the code, it always looked about the same with a script window, a preview window, and a properties window. I wrote code into the script window; when I ran the code, the results would appear in the preview window, and I could adjust the settings, properties, and parameters in the properties window.

From how Michel explained it, Think-Tree was similar, but the main-view was the preview window, taking up the majority of the screen, then the right side panel labeled properties was empty.

"I certed in biometrics and health coding."

"Okay, did you have your eyes set on the mental health project back then, too?"

With the helmet on her head, she shifted to get comfortable in the chair, leaning back into it. "No, I don't think I knew what I wanted to be."

Michel hummed. With the software set up, he clicked on the helmet icon to open the launch window. "Are you ready for me to turn the helmet on?" When she nodded, Michel tapped the green power button on the launcher, but turned back around to watch her. "Let me know if you need to take a break or we need to cut the connection."

Thalia nodded back as the helmet hummed to life.

I watched the screen where the status bar said tether loading. I didn't usually see any of this. I wasn't even sure why I was still there, except that it wasn't someone that came to Michel or knew Michel, it was someone I brought in. But even so, I wasn't really paying attention to Thalia, I was interested in the screen, the data.

Once the helmet had booted up and the software had synced to it, Michel would ask Thalia some guiding questions. Those questions would spur Thalia to think about certain things, and a mindscape would form in the preview pane on the screen. According to Michel, everyone's mind would preview differently, though there were some basic similarities. Some people's minds and memories would look like a timeline of events or a cause-effect chain. Some people's minds would come through in neat little folders or boxes. Some people would have multiple running banners of consciousness streaming at once. It was all different, but Michel would do the same thing with it for everyone, lead them to their own memories or their own conclusions, guide them to the answers they needed using the logic that their brain already ran on.

According to Michel, my brain looked like a simple queriable blockchain. He had described how beautiful and logical it was to me, how cute, which had dug straight into me. There was a part of me that wondered if Michel had led me directly into loving him, but if he had, then I was the luckiest man in the world.

Michel had a snippet of what part of his mind looked like, too. I wouldn't call it cute or beautiful, but I liked how symmetrical it was. I liked how the branches of the web reached out in a calculated way toward answers.

I was on the edge of my seat, waiting for Thalia to map her own mental processes.

Michel took a deep breath. "Hi Thalia, how are you feeling?"

Suddenly, the property pane was full of options. There were properties for pain and pressure and tightness, for joy and anger, for exhaustion and boredom, there was an entire subset of properties for taste. The selection for each property whirled through options, none of them legible. Michel waited patiently as they slowed to some static variables, ticking every once in a while, but I could read them before they switched.

Michel nodded to the calm property window. "Can you tell me about yourself? Kindergarten stuff, like your favorite food or your favorite color?" Michel watched the preview screen.

Nothing appeared in the window.

Michel's eyebrows furrowed. "Thalia, can you tell me about where you grew up or your parents' names?"

Still nothing.

Michel sat up straighter in his seat, eyes roving over the screen, opening menus across the software and checking the helmet's input settings. "Thalia, can you tell me about a friend of yours from primary school?"

When the screen preview remained blank, Michel's frustrated expression began to look worried. He flicked his eyes to me, like he was asking me something, to do something, but I didn't know what.

I wracked my brain, thinking of the cute little database posing a query, searching for relevant data, then connecting and transforming the data into an answer. I put a hand on Michel's thigh and cleared my throat. "Thalia, do you have any information on the Corporate Research Division's Mental Health Program?"

Michel rolled his eyes at me, but the screen changed, little dots appeared across the preview window. Michel forgot about me and went back to clicking through the menus, adjusting the preview size and the magnification.

Might as well keep going then, right? Right? "What were the results of the mental health check-in tests?" More dots appeared.

Zoomed in, we could see that the dots were little rectangular icons, but even at 700% size we couldn't make out what it was. Michel was digging deeper into the submenus trying to change the view. The screen updated to a close-up view.

These were files. There weren't folders or a logic system. They were files, laid out like they would be in a computer's file explorer.

Oh, Thalia.

I looked back to her, and I could see the tears trailing down her chin again. Her lips were pressed together, warbling slightly.

Michel gasped, shaking his head at the screen.

"Thalia, system user basic profile." It was the information that we stored in test data, so we could use basic demographics to qualify our findings.

The previewer jumped to another place on the visual, a single text file had appeared labeled *UserBasicProfile_Subject001_Hess,Thalia*.

Michel cut the tether and shut down the helmet. He took quick, little breaths as his fingers flew over the desktop. With everything disabled, he clicked the close button on the software. A pop-up asked him if he wanted to save the changes to the preview pane. He clicked no. A pop-up asked him if he wanted to save the changes to the software window. He clicked no. A pop-up asked him if he wanted to save the 0893_*Thalia,Hess_MentalMap* file.

I grabbed his hand.

He grimaced at me, and shook his head at me curtly. He clicked no.

I wasn't paid enough to care, and yet...

Michel removed the helmet from her head and hugged her while she ugly-cried into his shoulder. He looked torn and afraid. She looked wrecked.

"You should stay with us for a while." I said, realizing how serious I was after I'd already said it.

Grabbing her tighter, Michel nodded vigorously into the embrace. "We can figure this out."

IN TECHRADAR

Thoughts on mentalmAPP?

Posted by Margaret Yang, Coding Specialist and Techie
Reviewed by Bella Nickel, Alps Small Site Services
Posted 33 days ago, Last Edited 31 days ago

Lately, I've seen an influx of posts about the new mentalmAPP offering by various spas and clinics. I live in one of the tech-forward suburbs in the Greater-Greenville area and code for a living, but I'm skeptical about the new fad. My girlfriend thinks it could be worthwhile, seeing the way your brain sorts and processes information could be useful for breaking unwanted habits or getting out of a rut.

And, I do have to admit that I've been in a bit of a rut lately. I won't go into detail on this forum, since it isn't the place for it. What do people think of the service? Do you think it would be useful for this sort of application?

In your response, please volunteer A) if you've used the service, B) why you chose the service to begin with, C) whether it met your needs, and D) whether you think it could be useful for my purposes described above. Thanks!

108 Comments. Top 5 Comments below.

> Comment by Hulk Devros
> I have participated in the service. I used it as part of my behavioral therapy with NationAlive mental health care benefits. I don't think it would hurt, but interpreting the results without a trained professional can be tricky. I think it would definitely meet your needs, but I'd look for a specialty clinic that includes a trained therapist or consultant to explain the results.

> Comment by Michel Walker
> I have both been mapped and worked as a specialized mapping tech for several years. I think what you get out of any treatment depends on what you put into it. If you plan to dive deep into mapping and try to learn from the results, then I believe it can lead you to the change you're looking for.

Comment by Kimberly Trent, Flagged by 7 users, Cleared by Bella Nickel
I haven't been to a mapping facility, because my girlfriend keeps <u>hemming and hawing over it</u>! Lol. But while I'm here, what's the difference between the mentalmAPP and ThinkTree services? There is a local clinic that offers both, and I can't tell the difference.

Comment by Michel Walker, Response to Comment by Kimberly Trent
In short, ThinkTree is an older version of the software, back when it was controlled by its original designers, before it was assumed and reassigned by the Corporate Council. mentalmAPP is a newer release after it was acquired and rebranded by Alps. Hope this helps!

Comment by Kimberly Tent, Response to Comment by Michel Walker
It does! I'll prioritize the newer release over the older one. Gotta get all the new bells and whistles. Thanks!

ALPS SERVICE ANNOUNCEMENT

Posting, Moderating, Commenting, Sharing

Reviewed by Margaret Yang, Alps Technical Services
Posted 4 days ago, Last Edited 4 days ago

Alps is pleased to announce exciting changes in how you receive updates.

Posts you can trust

Posts will be ranked by a variety of factors to ensure that the posts and news that you care about hit your feed first. These factors include notoriety of source, poster rating, locality, and commentor relationship. Basically, we'll each see posts from people we know and trust in priority order.

Moderation streamlined

After receiving many complaints about the lag-time associated with forum moderation to enforce our posting terms and guidelines, we have streamlined the process.

Edits to posts will still be marked with the usual underline, but will no longer link directly to the moderation hub. Each author can access the moderation hub from their posting hub as the details become available.

Commenting as speech

Comments represent thought and engagement from real people, so the Alps reviewers will no longer be deleting or removing comments. You may have already noticed some moderators make this adjustment in their moderation. Going forward, the 'flag comment' button will phase out, making room for new and engaging options to roll on.

Sharing in real-time

Sharing is what we do best by introducing others to content and information that we find engaging or useful. New real-time sharing will allow users to share with each other quickly and easily. When you come across something that piques your interest and spurs you to conversation, you can choose to share with someone in a call format, sending an invite for the recipient to read the post and react on the line with you.

You can see the full list of updates at the application update log here.

Thank you for trusting Alps with your thoughts!